RED
STILETTOS

BY
RUTH JOSEPH

Published by Accent Press Ltd - 2004
ISBN 0954489977
Copyright © Accent Press Ltd 2004

Printed and bound by in the UK
by Clays Plc, St Ives

Cover Design by Scott Clark

DEDICATION

This book is dedicated to the special people in my life. My darling husband Mervyn who always believed in me and encouraged me, and my family: Sarah, my best audience, Joe my pal when life was tough, my son-in-law Darren, and Jasmine and Phoebe my most beautiful granddaughters and the inspiration for some of my stories.

Also very many thanks to Catherine Merriman. Her generous advice and encouragement have been invaluable. And of course my wonderful friends who have listened, teased and been proud of their friend.

ACKNOWLEDGEMENTS

'Patchwork' was previously published in *Ghosts of the Old Year* by Parthian in 2003 as a winner in the Rhys Davies Prize, and in the *Anthology of Contemporary Jewish Women's Writing* published in 2004 by Loki Books.

'Devon Cream' was published in *Mirror, Mirror* by Honno Welsh Women's Press May 2004.

'Mother of a Son' was published in *New Welsh Review* in Spring 2004.

'Stealing Baby' was the Lichfield and District 1st Prize Winner, 2004.

'Tapestry' was a Cadenza Prize Winner in 2004.

CONTENTS

TAPESTRY

I've twisted the night in hostile sheets. Is it only four a.m... then five? 'Don't worry... He'll be alright... It'll all be fine...'

The insistent cry of a bird shrieks through the curtained silk, stabbing the layers of darkness. Others begin to call. A flood of sound pours into the shadowy bedroom. No peace for me now. I look over at Joseph – one arm flung above his head, his mouth soft in sleep, eyes closed, edged with long black lashes. He's a good man. He would never let our child suffer... our baby... my son... first son. Eight days old.

I slide out of bed, the pain of stitches slicing my body, and shuffle my feet into sleeping slippers. Then walk stiffly like a King Penguin skirting an icy crevasse. Joseph stirs in the warmth of our bed. 'You OK?'

'Yes love... I'm fine... go back to sleep... It's gonna be a long day.'

I wrap my dressing-gown, hospital new, around my body. I'm grateful for its softness, comforting my shivers, and lean over the Moses basket at the end of the bed. Remember the arguments over who was going to buy it. Grandparents, aunties and uncles, all needing to share in such a pretty temporary arrangement. Within this organza'd wrapping of wicker and blue bows lies the object of my anxiety – a minute arrangement of diminutive limbs and organs contained in an overlarge baby-gro. In the early shadows I see a tiny face, new but already familiar: a part of Joseph, a part of me. Joseph's nose, my hands outstretched in unaccustomed freedom, like small pink stars with miniscule fingers, each perfect nail a miracle of creation. A thread in the fabric of our combined lives, a wholeness of mutual genes.

My breasts ache. In under an hour, Nathan will be crying and I will have to sit trying to be patient while he attempts to suck and I'll think of all the work to be done today – there's so much to do.

'Give it time,' said the visiting midwife. Silver watch hanging from efficient bosom. 'Give the milk time to come through. You're tired in the beginning and stressed.'

I shuffle my way downstairs. The clock welcomes with a familiar tick. My mind runs on numerous levels simultaneously, like Joseph's train set, now folded away in the loft and replaced by multi-packs of nappies, the cot, and a twirling mobile of pink and blue stuffed felt bunnies. The freezer mutters, protecting my anxious preparations – hours of labour waiting to be defrosted. Two hundred cocktail-sized fried gefilte fish balls, the same of salmon rissoles, and falafels, plus two hundred mini pizzas. Two hundred filo vegetable wraps... and chopped herring, hummus...

'You should have had a caterer,' said well-meaning friends. 'How can you possibly make the function and look after the baby and...'

'But I want it to be the best... I want to give my baby the best... the best I can do.'

I light a lamp near the bookcase and make a camomile tea, fighting off the urge for coffee – no good for the baby – and set my favourite mug on a table in the corner of the sitting room next to my tapestry. Pulled tight on the fancy stretcher he bought me for my birthday, hangs my own design etched on canvas. I was afraid to commemorate today, before it happened.

'G-d forbid!' they'd say. 'You'll give the baby an eyen horreh... the evil eye...'

'But I'm not superstitious!' I protest.

In the last few days I tried to finish it, feeling the low dull pains of pre-labour contractions, low in the belly and the back, wondering all the time, is this it? Is this what labour feels like? No rush, no rush to hospital. They all say to stay home on the first, until the pain gets too bad. I sat with cramped legs akimbo working frenetically with coloured silks and chunky cottons, to convey a sliver of time. Just a few stitches needed to finish. It's a kind of family tree with all our past generations surrounded by the flowers I grow in the garden and Joseph's new fruit seedlings.

As the pains grew I stayed with the threads, making a picture of our lives – the golden colours of bread, of wheat and grasses. The red deep claret of wine and grapes and Kiddush embellished with silver thread for candlesticks and menorah.

3

I need the therapy of my plants now to dispel nagging terrors. The kitchen door-lock clicks open easily and I venture outside into the coolness of leaves. It is late summer. The early morning drones heavy with the scent of honeysuckle and bees bumble busily, filling their pockets with nectar before the next rains. I walk down the small path Joseph and I laid together, down to the bottom where he fixed the seat under the gazebo. We laughed – it was such hard work. As I raise my head, the new dawn offers a watercolour sky, blush pinks and the fires of yellow gold. I sit surrounded by the stain of poppies, roses and geraniums – the colour of blood, and wine. Clashing purple foxgloves and wild rosebay willow herb, too pretty a weed to pull, spear the back of the border with their spires.

I carried the red of the poppies into my tapestry, but now, in the early morning – at a time of fears – the colours of the poppies and roses become the blood of my child, and the wine is not for the Sabbath and festivals but prescribed by the *mohel* to pacify his injured cries.

My gentile friends have argued with me, and their rubber-gloved operating theatre logic is strong in my mind.

'It's barbaric this way. At least get him done in a hospital, with an anaesthetic and doctors and nurses on hand. With respect, you must be crazy.'

Am I crazy? Am I mad? Why do I follow the traditions of my religion?

I leave my garden with its layers of sound and colour unfolding in the growing light, and pass the sleeping tapestry, back to our bedroom. Nathan is just stirring. He begins with a soft whimpering sound, which if left develops into high-pitched crying. But I try not to let that happen. I take this small infant out of his warm covers, change his nappy and, when he is clean, clutch his minuteness to my nakedness, enjoying the sweet scent of milky new skin. The down of his head nuzzles for my breast and makes loud slurping sounds which give me hope that I will feed him sufficiently.

Now I am physically contained but my thoughts run on like a hungry lioness tracking fresh scent of its quarry, urgent, relentless. What's the time? Half past five... and the *mohel* will be here at eleven. I tidied up last night and put away all the dishes. The glasses and the wine are out already... and I've taken the food out of the freezer and I want to put out some fruit, nuts, dill pickles. I busy myself with trivial domestic worries knowing these are not the focus of my fears. A surface diversion to avoid concentrating on the real terror of the day. My poor Nathan... my new baby... will he be... I stop myself. They call today a *simcha* – a reason to celebrate.

I remember I was only five when my cousin Chaim was *done*. The whole family was invited, my Mummy and Daddy and my two big brothers. I knew it was a special occasion because Mummy said I must wear my best Shabbat dress, the navy velvet with the white collar and my new black patent shoes with white tights. All the men gathered in the large front room. Many men with big black hats, singing and chanting like in *shool*. There was much talk about who was going to hold Chaim and which pillow to use and I'd heard that my Aunty Gloria had spent hours making something special. Then she showed us the pillow. It was so beautiful, new, white and soft like the feathers of a swan, edged with lace and decorated with scrolls of dark and light blue ribbon. The singing got louder and louder and I was bored with the ladies so I slipped away from Mummy. Nobody noticed. They were too busy putting cups on saucers and arranging doilies on plates to see that I had gone. They had left the door open because there were a lot of people and the room was hot. I'd always sat with Daddy. He let me stay with him in *shool* if I was really quiet. I wanted to see the pillow. Why was it so important and what were they going to do to Chaim? Thick coats, black thick coats, navy coats, many many legs in trousers and navy shoes, black shoes and where was Daddy? Then I saw the pillow – saw Chaim laid on the pillow without his nappy and the man using a metal cutting thing on Chaim's...

Daddy was cross. Said I spoilt the occasion for everyone being sick like that. I should have stayed with Mummy. It was the blood on Aunty Gloria's pillow. Why were people so happy?

I brush away an angry tear and put my child over my shoulder to wind him. He's a good little boy. Taken his feed and is sleeping again. I leave him with Joseph in our bedroom and make my way downstairs to my domestic trivia. And I reason with myself. *It's a long time ago, girl, since you were a child. You know these men are so well qualified.* Joseph comes down with our sleeping child in his arms. 'He can sleep downstairs now in the pram. Later, I'll go and get the Moses basket... take a few minutes break. Go on, have some tea and toast... watch the television for a while. There's ages before they all come.' He lays little Joseph in his pram and I hear the rattle of the kettle lid and the click of the toaster.

6

Just a few more stitches. I would love to finish the tapestry before Aunty Gloria comes. I wouldn't let her see it until it was finished. She'll walk in with Uncle Harry, in a dress adorned with vast shocking pink overblown roses, or yellow spots on green. She loves her colours and I love her spirit. It doesn't matter that her taste is loud – her heart is as large as her decorative spirit. She will appreciate the tapestry. I could finish... only a few stitches. I move over to the needlework that spans the waiting hours of my pregnancy and concentrate. I am the spider that spins the web of ideas and forms them into a design. I thread a silver thread, and weave a decoration on the Kiddush *becher* – the silver beaker they will drink from at the ceremony. The same silver is woven into the tops of the candlesticks. I am the weaver that sees the glint of moonbeams on water and turns them into diamonds. But I am also weaving a tapestry of souls. My past and my future, together with my family's. I weave in their names, those of the past, and soon my child, and then he will become part of what we are. I am a follower of tradition.

I won't put in Nathan's name yet. But after today... a few days to recover... please God when all is well, I will include his name.

'It's time, love... ' Joseph says. Did I drop off for a minute? Can that be possible with so much happening today? I slip past the pram, carefully allowing little Nathan his last quiet minutes, and change quickly into a simple dress which will be deemed respectful in the eyes of the clergy. It is grey, modestly cut with sleeves to the elbow, and flows loosely about my legs. Then return for Nathan to change him.

I can hear voices downstairs. Uncle Josh's booming tones, Aunty Cissie's high pitched squeak and groups of nosy ladies checking the kitchen to view the catering arrangements and whether I've managed. Joseph runs up the stairs. 'Stay up here, there's no need for you to come down until it's over.' Then he whisks away my baby.

I am cold. I wipe clammy hands against my skirt. Feel the knock of my heart banging in the cavern of my chest. I can hear the chanting and the singing and my stomach squeezes with the pain that Jewish mothers have felt since time began. Why did I let them? Why should it be so? Can that tiny child, only eight days old, bear the agony of such an operation? Joseph returns, it seems, hours later. My face is flooded with tears. The front of my dress is wet with milk leaked for my child. My tiny son lies on a pillow. On his miniature face is one small tear, but he is quiet, almost sleeping.

'Is he alright? Why isn't he crying?'

'He had a good swig of wine just at *that* moment. The *mohel* was very good. Very quick and efficient. When you've fed Nathan, wash your face, change and meet your family and your friends. You wanted to show Aunty Gloria the tapestry. You were going to show her today.'

My child feeds from my breast. Large slurping sounds as before. I stroke the soft down on his head with one finger and press my mouth in silent kisses all over his body. Then I change him. He has a large bandage and plaster over the wound. But he does not seem distressed. I put on an ordinary skirt and blouse, the milk-stained party outfit discarded for the wash.

Then, after checking the baby monitor, I descend to meet the noise that swells up the stairs.

'Mazaltov, my dear... a very special occasion. Now your son is one of us. He has been given his Jewish identity,' says Mr Samuels with his mouth full of chopped fried gefilte fish. 'You must have worked so hard,' they chorus. 'How did you manage to make all that food?'

'I hedged my bets... I'd make a party anyway, boy or girl. It's easy with a freezer... ' I make my excuses. My mind is upstairs in that cot. Aunty Gloria clacks over, the mass of her large body balanced on four-inch stilettos. She's dabbing her eyes. 'Such a wonderful occasion, I know, darling, it's always a bad day for the mother. But that's the way it is with us'

I don't want to talk. I am too full of emotion. 'Would you like to see the tapestry?'

'Not today, sweetheart. I'll come again in a week or two when you are more settled.'

I'm grateful for her thoughtfulness and soon they all pick up coats fallen like abandoned bodies over the couch in my small sitting room and the house returns to two people plus one, a multitude of sticky dishes and glasses, and a smell of herring and wine.

We eat with our minds resting on that small child, upstairs, and after he cries and I feed him, I bring him down, freshly changed, smelling of milk.

'Let's go out in the garden,' I say. 'I'll wrap him up well.'

Joseph walks ahead of me down the path we both constructed holding his son and singing quietly. He sits on our seat and beckons for me. Their two heads are close, my two Jewish men. They sit by the red of my poppies and roses and I smell the dusk perfumes of all my flowers. Liquid songs of blackbirds reverberate from the tips of the highest trees.

I think of how it is, of how the day progressed. Today this child who has no past was blessed by his ancestors. They watched him. They stood by him, holding hands, keeping him safe, as he was given his Jewish identity. Their ideals and dreams have been woven into the fabric of his life as I embroidered them in the tapestry of our lives. He walks with the famous. Maybe he could be as clever as Einstein, or as artistic as Claude Pissarro or Amadeo Modigliani. Possess the musical talents of Felix Mendelessohn or Max Bruch. He has had his debut. Now, he has a past, is our present, and has his singular future. He will tread in our footsteps – in our history.

Joseph raises the wrapped body of his little son to the golden light in some kind of private homage.

'It's getting cold, my little family. Let's go in,' he says. 'It went well... didn't it?'

Then walks me, slowly, back to the house.

DEVON CREAM

'Barbara. You've got to promise, just promise you'll come over tomorrow for lunch. You can...? Yes I know I sound... I had some dreadful news yesterday. Yes it will wait... but now there's the teapot... Yes a drink would be good idea... in a while... after the children have left... I promise... I promise... I'll... You will come... won't you...? Yes, about one. Great ... OK love... I'll see you tomorrow...'

I put the receiver down and look at the dustpan filled with fragments of china teapot. Impossible to glue it back together. Remember what it looked like: large, elaborate Victorian. Like her, stiff-legged, reigning on its own stand. You daft thing, I chide myself. It's just a bloody tea-pot. Hideous thing. I was only moving it off the top of the display cabinet so that when the children came for the party it would be safe. It's just that after receiving the post yesterday morning – I must try to get things into proportion. It's not a mirror that's broken. It's Gerald's mother's tea-pot. It belonged to her grandmother before her. He was terrified of that old woman. No, correction, he hated her, the witch. She lived in one of those old miners' cottages at the top of the valley. She wore a black gown down to her ankles, even when the fashion changed to short, and a black knitted shawl hugged around thick shoulders. Before my time, but I've seen the photos often enough. Small woman but solid, with pit-prop thighs. Born with sobriety springing through her veins, and an intolerance of those who indulged in the slightest drop – even at Christmas. When he was a child and had to pass her house to get to school, he'd cross the road, or sneak right under her doorway, but she always saw him, and then she'd scream:

'What have you done wrong that you're trying to avoid me?'

Her own grandson, for goodness sake! That bony finger would poke his chest and he'd shake for hours after. He told me. And then when she died, it was as if his mother moved into her tight, black, lace-up shoes and smack into our lives. Like a dose of black poison, that's what she was like – Satan's pee.

I try to push vindictive sinful thoughts out of my mind and return to my preparations for the children's Halloween party. I've promised them one for years. But the witch stopped it and then a myriad of problems prevented me. But this year is going to be different.

I remember, two years ago, the last time I tried to organize one of these parties, she screamed that it was a blasphemous occasion, a Witches' Sabbath, and she hadn't taken Gerald to church for all those years so he could play witchcraft games with his children. Then she had one of her asthma fits. I'm sure she did it deliberately, and instead of the children having a few friends over and dressing up, trick or treating, Gerald and I ended up at the hospital with her. There she was gasping for oxygen, and me wondering how we always did what she wanted. One way or another she always got her way.

I put on a piece of music, and get out the sugar and the margarine. Start beating them together, and whipping the eggs, and at last the kitchen begins to feel comforting, and warm, and some of my frustration begins to ebb. I add a little green colouring to the cake mixture, and it looks suitably gruesome. Then I drop teaspoons of the mixture into paper cases, and pop them in the oven. But I can't resist peeping at them through the glass door, as they rise. That green shade makes them look disgusting – the kids will love them. I've par-boiled potatoes and cut them into wedges plastering them with olive oil and barbecue spice and there's a stack of sausages waiting in a roasting tin. I'll do some chocolate crispies, and decorate them with liquorice bats I found in Tesco, and I've planned to make a pot of roasted pepper and chilli soup with bread, and then we'll be done. I can't see the harm. The children know it's only fun. The real thing, the real witch, is the one that hung about my house like a dark cloud and reduced Gerald to a state of soggy blotting paper. And where is she now?

Don't think about her. Concentrate on the weeks ahead and try to put that woman out of your mind. Fat chance with that parcel sitting outside in the shed and the tea-pot smashed to bits.

The cakes are cooked. They smell delicious. What a strange colour. When they're cool, I'll decorate them with small worms I've made out of marzipan. I've put currants on them for eyes. I've a lot to make up for. The children have had a tough time – all their lives really. I think of Bethan's birth and how terribly she behaved. She was staying with us then, only for a few months, on and off, just until the breathing became better. Gerald was worried about her attacks, and it was easier to have her in the house than have to drive over in the middle of the night, after a three-o-clock-in-the-morning panic phone-call. I had to go in for a week before the birth – something to do with my blood pressure, and I'd prepared all the food for the time that I would be away, including hers. Admittedly there were a few prepared meals bought from Tesco, but very few. And anyway, Gerald likes their burgers. I used to get them specially. Apparently she ranted about how I didn't bother, and how in her day they never used junk food. Of course they didn't – there wasn't any. While I was in hospital, unbeknown to me, she moved in to my house. Permanently. She brought over all her possessions in a small orange hire-van with a driver. Strange how she managed to do all that without having one asthma attack. Each time he came to visit me, Gerald wore a dreadful expression as if someone was tearing his skin with sharp nails. When I came home I knew why.

Everything had been moved or changed. Gerald just stood there as I walked through my home. He tried to smile as I looked at my ornaments, shoved into a corner, and that bloody teapot in pride of place. A large black crucifix on a nail had been hammered into the wall, over the mantelpiece. I had to sit in the kitchen, weak from the birth, blood loss and stitches, pushing back the tears. She had turned my house into hers. It was now a replica of the place I hated. I opened one drawer. It was lined with crackle-stiff greaseproof, and a large air-freshener had taken the place of my plants on the windowsill.

'My plants?' I said. 'Where are my plants?'

'All dead,' said Gerald, still with that agonized expression. The witch stood behind, with the hint of a smile pulling at her mouth. I could smell her triumph like a hidden slime.

'Why don't you take your things off, upstairs, while I make us all a cup of tea?' she said, and leaned over in her moment of victory, to look at the baby.

'Dear me, I hope she's alright. That child looks very pale to me.'

I moved upstairs, holding my little one close, and into our bedroom. Everything had changed. It was repainted blue! When I'd left the room, just a week ago, it was a soft pink. I heard her move beside me.

'Not a nice idea to let a man sleep in a pink room, is it, love? Maybe you hadn't thought of that. So I freshened it up for you. It was to give you a bit of a surprise, a welcome home present.'

Our bed a commodious double, two singles zipped together, and it was now rent in two, one of the bedside tables between. Above our heads was another crucifix. I have never been a person who shows her anger. It's not my way. I can't do it. I soak up the damage and pain like a mucky rag doused in acid, burning on the inside. And I suppose, I was young then, afraid to speak, and I wasn't strong. Remember, I was just out of hospital. How I managed to get out of our bedroom and into the nursery, I'll never know. But I was not going to let her see my tears.

15

'Got to see to the baby,' I muttered, and held her tight in my arms away from that woman's clutches. I made for the nursery, the lemon sanctuary decorated with characters from Winnie the Pooh. Thank the Lord, nothing had changed here. I sat down gingerly on the small nursing chair Gerald and I had positioned ready for my homecoming. Gerald had placed a small bunch of lily of the valley from the garden in a small blue glass vase, next to the cot. I fed my child and irrational ideas flowed with my milk. I thought of doing everything, from poisoning her just enough to keep her in hospital, to leaving Gerald. What kind of man allows his mother to destroy his marriage? But in the end I knew that I would cope with her evil. I would make this place of child sighs and milky scents my sanctuary, and escape from the witch.

It's a long time ago now, but the memories are painful. Life with her never improved. She interfered in our lives, and the lives of our children. Sometimes she'd seem like she was trying to be kind, and, like a fool, I'd fall for it. The bitterest moment was when she insisted we went to Gerald's school friend's wedding. We were two days away. By the time we came back, she'd banned old Jess to a place under the sink in the scullery and destroyed all her blankets. She'd started having the odd accident in her old age and left ponds of urine. I knew then that I would never trust that witch with anything I loved, and that she would always try to hurt us.

Two nights ago we went to a pre-Halloween 'do' for the children's school, at our local coffee-shop. We were promised a woman who'd tell our fortunes from our coffee grounds. I didn't know that sort of thing existed. Thought it had to be tea leaves. Gerald was keen, he said it would be good to get out and meet people. Well, there she was, "Lady Branwen", draped in the obligatory purple chiffon plastered with stars, like Merlin's apprentice, and I had to fight off the giggles. We were all queuing up for a reading. You had to use coffee that was not strained and most of the grounds went to the bottom. Then you had to drink as much as possible, cover the cup with the saucer, and swirl it around three times in a clockwise direction. Then allow the whole thing to settle. "Lady Branwen" looked grave when she read my cup.

'I don't like giving readings that could be worrying, but you've got a classic dagger. Well, a knife anyway,' she said.

'What does that mean?' I asked 'Please tell me.'

'Sorry, the standard answer is that there is some kind of danger ahead. But it could just be something small. Don't worry... I'm sure it's not terrible news.'

But I was shocked. Since the witch's death we'd all been so happy, the best we'd ever been. She'd died three months before. She'd decided to take off on a grand holiday to Australia. She wanted to see her daughter, the one who must really have loved her, because she rang every Friday without fail. She had fallen ill there, died and was cremated. So my personal thorn could do no more damage.

When we got home, Gerald laughed that I'd taken the reading seriously.

'Oh, come on, love, it's a few coffee grounds. Nothing's going to happen.'

Until the post arrived the next morning.

The children's party is over. It was a huge success. But I can't get an image out of my mind. Afterwards, I took a walk through the country lanes, just by the house, and saw a group of ravens sitting like black-gowned judges on the branches of an oak tree that had lost most of its leaves. The pale sun looked tired as if it knew it only had a few hours before sleep.

Barbara arrives promptly at one. I hug her with wired fingers.

'Do you mind if I show you something first?' I say. 'Before we eat.'

'No love... What's the matter? Where are we going?'

'To the apple store,'

'Mm... lovely,' she says. She's always liked the smell of that place, of the ripening apples. Like a vat of fresh cider, she says, rich as breathing. We walk through the warmth of the kitchen, past my table laid with bread and salad, past the Aga, where a pot bubbles with a vegetable stew, to the chill of outside and the stone out-house. The door moves with a creak. Spiders' webs hanging from the stone lintels of the door cling to our faces as we push it open and enter the gloom. The apple scent has changed and a sweet, sour scent of rottenness hangs in the air. I scan the shelves, where each apple is carefully wrapped and sleeping in its own tissue bed. Maybe one of them is on the turn. Then I turn to my friend and show her a large Jiffy bag covered in postage stamps. I can feel the colour draining from my face.

'It's mother-in-law,' I say,

'What do you mean?'

'She's in here. In this bag posted from Australia. She wants to be scattered over our garden. She liked the meadow and the views so she wants to – I can't have it in the house. I'll have to do it soon. Scatter the bloody stuff and I'm afraid that if the children find out...'

I pass the bag to Barbara to hold and I can see her face. She's gagging as she returns it, but trying to hide her disgust, hoping not to hurt my feelings. I lay it on one of the shelves and we run back to the warmth of the kitchen. But I'm bone-bitter chilled. I make an excuse, dash to the toilet and scrub my hands, again and again, grateful for my nail-brush. Then I return, and dish out portions of stew with bread. It's a brandy I need.

'For goodness sake! How did that happen? You hated her, didn't you?'

'Yes. She was cruel and she treated me badly. All of us. She interfered in everything, made trouble with the children and between me and Gerald. When she went to live with my sister-in-law in Australia, I was so delighted. Then she died and I was rid of her forever. Glory be! Now she's back. When we scatter her remains the bloody dust will be in my garden where I work every free moment. She'll be in the seeds, in the roots of the trees, sticking in my throat on a dry day...'

'Can't you scatter her on the slope at the far end of the garden... and maybe you can grow more brambles on that patch?' But she looks at my face and my shaking whiteness.

'You see – she's come back to haunt me and no matter what I do she's going to be here – forever.'

'Oh no, she's not coming back here.' Barbara pushes back her plate on the table and gets up. 'Leave the food now. Cover up the plates. We'll eat later. We've got to sort out this witch. I've got an idea. But we'll have to be quick. We'll take my car.'

'What?'

'We have to make the old witch suffer. A kind of hell on earth. Then you can start enjoying your life again. Right. No time to lose. Gruesome job first. Get out the liquidizer!'

'Liquidiser...!'

'Right, where's the new bag of cat litter kept? I know you bought a spare one.'

'Underneath the sink. But what do you want with...'

'Wake up, goose! They've sent her from Australia. You'll still have to scatter something, won't you? They'll want all the details. Maybe even a photo. And Gerald. You must never tell Gerald, or the children. It's our secret.'

I stare, mesmerized, as Barbara opens the new bag of cat litter and spoons mound after mound of the grey lumpen mass into the machine. Then with a deep chuckle that rises from her belly, she cries:

'Switch on, switch on. The new ashes are about to be conceived.'

Laughing, we shake the grey dust into a polythene bag.

'Yuk. Now for the really gruesome bit.'

She takes another large bag, the office stapler, and a mixing spoon out of my storage pot, grabs our coats and pushes me towards the apple store.

'I'm not sure I...'

'Yes you bloody can...'

'Yes I can,' I say. 'You're right... Whatever... OK.'

The wind smacks at our faces and we are both shivering as we enter the apple store. Can't breathe. Can't breathe. My heart is thudding all over my body as Barbara carefully prises the staples from the Jiffy bag. I need to be sick. Halloween images and the fortune teller's daggers flood my mind. Will some ghostly harpy released from Hades jump out and... those bony digits. But Barbara has the Jiffy bag open now and is tipping the contents into our spare bag. Then she shakes the cat litter powder into the Jiffy bag and restaples it.

'First stage over,' she breathes and leans against one of the stone walls. 'Right, quickly!'

We're in her car bumping over frozen country lanes, and I'm clutching a mixing spoon and a polythene bag of... holding it at a distance.

'Hang in there, girl. You can do it. Just to the pub.'

The small car thunders down the roads. It's now early evening and, as we drive, tree silhouettes materialize into demoniac shapes. Limbs reach out to scrape the windscreen.

'Why the pub? You know how she disapproved of drinking.'

'Exactly! Be as quiet as possible when we arrive. OK? She looks at me with a satisfied smirk. 'You know they always have a Halloween party on the night, and there are always a few daft fools or kids who throw a few eggs or worse on the walls. Well, next day Mark always gets a few lads in to give all the walls a coat of textured paint. And I know where they've put it.'

She drives to the pub. We park. All is silent. We get out of the car, not shutting the car door and walk around the corner. There by the kitchen door sits a stack of paint-pots, some already opened, with brushes and rollers. Smothering giggles, we remove two of the tins. Then, in the gloom of the boot, we mix in the ashes. The name on the side of the tin is Devon Cream, Texturised Paint. We replace the tins with the others. And drive away, hooting like the possessed.

We're back in my kitchen, at the table. The dark looks in and watches us – two women laughing, drinking wine and eating stew. It all tastes so good.

'She's gone from here forever,' says Barbara, 'and each time you go the pub, you'll be able to raise your glass to the old witch, stuck on all the pub walls, in the place she hated the most. Toast "Devon Cream", and smile.'

PAYING FOR IT

And did you know, when we began, when you first came to the flat, the shoulders of your cream linen suit drenched with a sudden spring shower, your eyes clouded with the hurt of the city and your lips seamed tight with unsaid words? Did you know then that you could shuffle the Tarot of our lives with a flick of your needs?

I heard your footsteps following the turn of the stairs. You paused. Then hit the black painted wood with your fist, over and over. I opened the door.

'There's a bell on the side here. Look.'

You walked into my space and your eyes flicked lizard-like assessing my possessions, calculating my status.

'How much?' you said, your left hand clutching a bunch of cellophane-wrapped flowers – gaudy yellow and orange – the offerings of a late-night garage. You threw the blooms on my chair, the old one covered

23

with my grandmother's embroidered Turkish shawl. They slipped and fell, breaking a few heads on the lino. I knelt to rescue the remaining blossoms and, as I rose, I caught your eyes, chiaroscuro, melting into the shadows. You wore an expression that reminded me of Tusker, John the Big Issue seller's mongrel, cowering on the wet concrete pavement. I pretended not to see.

'I do French... ' I began monotonously, like reciting my five times table.

'No no... no... ' You shook your head and waved notes – many notes.

'Do what you can with this,' you said.

I was glad. I hate the money bit. They all think that's the reason why. But it's not. You took me with anger in your hands and your body was coiled and tight like an over-strung guitar. Then, when you were done, you lay on your back and breathed deeply. I watched your face, saw the tight mouth soften, unseen wires in your hands release their grip. Something inside persuaded me to relax my guard; for some reason I broke the rules. I'd made it a commandment not to get involved, an absolute law: to get up, get dressed and *move 'em out* like they say in the westerns. Never let them get to you. Damn it. I never did. But I lay next to you. Skin to skin, under the black satin. I broke the rules, my rules. My hand stretched to touch the soft hairs at the top of your belly. Then I ran my fingers up your chest. You flinched as if my touch was a lit cigarette on your flesh. I felt your body shudder and you turned and looked at me with those clouded eyes. I knew there was pain and I wanted to ease it. Why?

My fingers brushed your lips. You moved closer so that our faces were inches away and your eyes closed, your mouth longing for kisses. But I never kiss unless I love. The other part – the part below the waist – can stay detached. Most of the time, the ones that visit are so pent-up, anxious, well, desperate, that in seconds it's all over, and I pretend I've come with them. A few oohs and aahs suffice. But I never give them my mouth.

'Can I stay?' you whispered. 'Please... ?'

Usually it's easy. *That'll be a hundred or two hundred or three.*

'What do you fancy... a massage... a rub in the shower?'

You stopped me. Laid tanned fingers on my lips. 'Just your arms... hold me...'

As the night began to lose its momentum, you rose. You didn't bother with a sheet to wrap like some of the others. I lay and watched – observed the lean of your back ebb into perfect spheres. I wanted to draw you. Cover canvas and paper with your image. You walked with ease and confidence, possessing the world, like a child who knows and loves a mother and a father. Moving from the soft red light surrounding my bed to my tired blind, you opened my window. It answered with a creak. Outside sounds of a city fighting sleep floated into our space. Below, an ambulance screamed its way through the narrow street.

A voice inside my head urged me to pull on my clothes. Pop the crisp white banknotes into my purse. Be brisk... be firm... be business-like. But instead I gazed, dream-like, as your hand stretched out to me.

'Come by the window. Let me look at you in the light.'

I wished for a moon. I wanted you to see me in the shivering brightness of the silver disc. But I have no view of the sky: just tall buildings crushing my sight, flashing their wares with neon fire. Strobe-speed, my body changed from shocking pink and violet, to blue, to almost black – a chameleon figure vibrating into colour, then into black. Then I became a watcher, watching you – a shadow, then a shadow on a shadow – hearing only your voice.

'You are so...'

Your fingers ran down my curves, over my breasts, pale black, my violet thighs. I tried to return to my sanity, to my rules. I could hear Scarlet, the next day at the café, dragging on a wisp of a roll up tight in its silver holder. *Don't give in. Keep yourself to yourself. You'll get hurt.* In my mind, her face was clear of its night make-up to reveal its death-mask ivory. Her arms purplish–blue, scarred with the passion for the tourniquet and needle – her secret communion with the anti-Christ. She sat drumming her fingers, dancing to inner voices that never ceased.

Don't tell him your thoughts, she would say. *Don't let them into your mind. They pay for the rest, but shut off your brain. That's your safety – that's your privacy!*

Then I looked up at you. You placed your arms around my shoulders and led me to my little table in the corner of the room. I'd placed a small stone Buddha on a saffron silk sari and behind it a silver-plated menorah – the nine-branched candlestick. Beside them both, an art nouveau copper vase I found in a flea market. I'd filled it with sticky buds bursting their shiny cases, and a few dried honesty stems, their opalescent seeds shimmering like flattened pearls against my crushed-velvet curtains. To the side of my mini-shrine rested my easel and canvas covered with a damp cloth, waiting for their time with me.

'What's all this? Artist... Buddhist... Jewish?'

I wiggled my nakedness. 'Split personality?' I joked. But I was afraid of those eyes – cool green, the colour of a quarry of my childhood, fathoms deep, of the waters of the Arno in Verona after heavy summer rains. I knew their capabilities, their power to dip into my soul, unpick the seams of my thoughts, find threads, discover, know secrets. Your eyes would race tickertape-quick through my remembrance. Staring starving people, striped coats, white and green faces, black numbers needled into paper wrists, barbed wire with sharpened steel teeth sucking at empty flesh. Floodlights and fear, the scream of dogs trained to kill. Boots, marching boots, polished boots kicking into wizened flesh, and always... always the smell of death. Bury the vision in the pile of suitcases, never let them know. Lock in the pictures...

They found out in school. Made a ring of arms and danced around me.

'Your granny slept with a gipsy. Yah Yah, your mum's a bastard child. She was born in a field and you were made in a ditch. You're worm food.

Yah yah, your mum's a hippy junkie and your dad went a walking playing his guitar...'

I was five, when my mother explained. I needed to understand. She wanted to justify, though the words floated through the scented smoke of another spliff.

'Coffee...?' I asked you, afraid of the questions, feeling the chill of outside pouring over my body.

'You're cold,' you said and leaned over to shut out the brightness. As you banished the dawn, shivers

27

shook my body. Your arms encircled mine. I felt small and unusually precious.

'You're not the usual type of... '

I tried to return the conversation to safety. Talk about tricks, massage, blows, anything to slip into the familiar. But you lifted up my jaw with your finger so that my face looked into yours. I stared into your light green with my black.

'I don't want you as a... ' He stopped the words. 'Just talk... I'd like to get to know you better.' I pulled my chin out of your grasp, thoughts brooding.

You have your own people, why me? I wondered, but left the words floating in the air, mixing with the sandalwood incense.

Morning came. I watched ribs of light pour over your forehead and illuminate the furrows of your life. Your mouth muttered business anxieties. I slid my body out of your gentle grasp and abandoned our cocktail of luxurious warmth, wrapping myself in my red brocade kimono – a present from a far eastern client. I made coffee and toast. You heard the kettle and woke with a start, for a second disorientated. Then I saw you breathe feelings of peace. You lay back.

'Can I come back tonight?' you asked. 'I want to know you... to discover why. Why have you made a shrine to two religions? Can I see your paintings?'

'I need to love,' I said. 'As for the rest, maybe sometime I will tell you.'

By then I wanted to give you a place in my world. Even in my mind. But not yet, and tonight, I would still be fearful. Not anxious about your fingers or the urgency of your body, but about your probing words.

Then you glanced at your watch and I saw the hurt of your other life return.

'I've got to go,' you muttered. Snakes of anxiety twisted your face.

'No more time. I'll come tonight at eight ...?'

You touched my lips. In seconds you were dressed and gone. I heard your footsteps descend and leaned out of the window. You ran across the street and disappeared. I reheated the contents of the cafetiere and sat for a while remembering the feel of your strong arms – tasting the scent of your body.

I had to save that emotion, to seal you within a painting – like a pubescent kid with a new pop star on her wall. I searched through my canvases. Money had been short – all my blank boards gone. Then I looked at my last work – an effort to understand my grandmother's agonies and my mother's wasted existence. Maybe it was right to put you in, as part of now. I worked fast with heavy brushwork and a pallet knife: vibrant tones in primary colours, cadmium reds, cadmium yellow, ochres and my saffron yellow. Then I remembered Scarlet. She would be waiting.

On the street it seemed as if the day had been drawn with re-sharpened crayons. The colours were vivid, acute. For the moment, the sky was an intense blue. Yesterday's showers had washed the pavements and the fruit and the vegetables on the market stalls were brilliant with life. Red peppers, yellow and green, looked polished and laid out, it seemed, as offerings to the gods. Massive purple aubergines yearned to be chopped into Mediterranean stews, whilst pale leafy fronds dressed the pink new season's rhubarb with delicate frills. A thought chased through my mind. *Should I cook for him?* But he was not my partner or boyfriend. He was a client. I sensed Scarlet's disapproval. And ran to the café at the end of the street.

She sat under her personal cloud. Somehow, that morning, I could not be patient. I was always sympathetic. I knew she was bound by the rhythm of the needles, the constant beat of the want-and-need drums. But only yesterday I'd seen her pimp who was also her supplier, arriving in his bronze and gold Mercedes – cream Armani suit and matching cream Fedora tip-tilted, a mirror image of a forties movie star. After his visits I always witnessed new needle marks and sometimes she would show me fresh bruises. And then she'd parade a new pair of croc stilettos or a black designer dress that ached on the curves of her body.

She was slumped in our usual corner dig–digging the sugar with a stabbing beat, tied and bound by the involuntary movements of her own internal pulse. She watched me out of the corner of her eye.

'All night eh... hope you made him pay plenty!'

'Yes... yes, love. He's paying... but I like him.'

'Like him,' she scorned. Her animated fingers forced and jabbed, holding the spoon in a clenched fist like a small tin dagger.

'You can't trust any of them. They're all shit. They're there to pay and fuck, just pay and fuck and then bugger off.' She spat on the floor.

Usually I listened. I understood the words spoken in her language. But today I couldn't pay attention. I drank a quick coffee, hugged her emaciated shoulders, then made an excuse and walked back to the market engrossed in my thoughts.

'Fancy a bit of fruit, darling?' Mike shouted.

I laughed and pointed to a dark purple onion, a vast aubergine, magenta-shiny, two strong firm

30

courgettes, a yellow and a red pepper and a bag of firm tomatoes still redolent with fragrance in their prickly stalks. The bag was awkward and as I struggled to prise one of the notes from the wad, Mike shouted 'Gor blimey girl you must be good! If my missus gives me time off for good behaviour, I'll come and treat myself to a few minutes with you!'

I was still smiling as I chopped the onions and set them to sizzle with some olive oil in a large pan. An urgent knocking startled me. I rushed to the door thinking it must be Scarlet in trouble again. In those seconds my mind was dealing with accidents at casualty, blood, vomit and new stitches, or, as she looked this morning, maybe another attempted suicide. But it was you.

'Why are you here now? You said tonight at eight.'

'I couldn't wait. Please forgive me. I needed... '

You carried a large pomegranate – a traditional Jewish fertility symbol – and a bottle of Chianti. You moved into my room and placed the pomegranate on my small table next to the stone Buddha. Left the bottle on the floor, then turned. Once again I felt your hurt. And you were in my space. I was in your arms, forgetting my rules, abandoning safety.

You carried me gently over to the bed. This time you were the lover. I was your loved one. You lay me on the black satin. Then lay beside me. I watched as you peeled off your jacket.

'Stop, stop!' I laughed. A smell of caramelised onions roused my conscience. 'I must switch off the pan.'

'Sorry... . looks like you're preparing for someone. I... I shouldn't have just barged in... wanted to see you again... the bloody screen on the PC... ' Your voice trailed away.

'It's OK,' I answered. 'I was making this for you.' I pushed Scarlet's parchment face firmly out of my mind. You never asked me why I was cooking for you.

After, a long time after, I rose to make jasmine tea. I felt your eyes tasting my body as I added the rest of the chopped vegetables and a handful of herbs to my rescued onions, boiling some water for pasta. Then you stood next to me. We were a couple, stirring the pot, making the meal together: you in your nakedness, me in mine. I drained the pasta carefully and topped it with the vegetables. You opened the bottle of Chianti but your eyes never left my body.

We sat eating opposite each other, twirling pasta on animated forks, sucking the red herby juices. You fed me with a forkful of your pasta and a drop of red liquid fell on my breast. Your fingers brushed my skin and your mouth tasted me. No words until we'd finished. Then I heard the intake of your breath.

'Can I see your paintings? Please... '

You moved over to the canvas that was masked by my damp cloth.

'I would love to... '

I heard Scarlet cursing

You peeled back the damp cloth and the scent of turpentine and linseed oil chased away the herby scents. You gasped as you saw my grandmother's Belsen face intertwined with the ghost of her gipsy lover and my mother's wistful eyes, starved of mother love, drowning in seas of futile dreams. Then you saw yourself, as I imagined you – a part of my future.

And did you know when we began, that our destinies were coupled – foretold like the kiss of neon on black velvet, the rich pour of claret into glass, and the slick of linseed-scented paint on canvas.

You did not flinch, my darling. You saw my truth and still wanted me. You arrived with anger in your heart, just another client, but still treated me with respect.

After, in that moment when emotions lie vulnerable, exposed on the twisted sheets, you still behaved as if you loved me. I was your lady.

I am your lady.

INTO THE CORNFIELD

So she says in a rush, 'Please Mum. You will make the cake won't you? And you won't put one of those ghastly brides and grooms on the top that look as if they're bored with each other already, will you?'

'What would you like darling?' I say, prepared for anything these days.

'And not flowers. They're so dated!'

I look at this woman, my daughter, her face flushed with excitement, her tiny hands replicas of mine, but smaller, challenging the air with fired conversation, long, sable curls bouncing on animated shoulders.

'What do you want, darling?' I ask.

'Well, we thought of Teddies...'

'Oh fine', I say. 'Yes, darling... Yes, of course...'

'Can you believe it?'

I sit with Margaret, pouring tea into the bone china mugs – the good ones for visitors. A leisurely lunch. Marg and I have been friends for over twenty years. We don't count them any more. She and I have seen it all. Absentmindedly she breaks off a piece of my home-made granary bread and dips it into the pot of hummus. A dog barks faintly in the background. The kitchen clock ticks slowly, no rush. Our time. A whole afternoon.

'Teddies,' she laughs. 'After all you have been through. How extraordinary.'

I didn't taste the tea, hear the words, but saw the child. Saw the baby born with difficulty, out of a prolonged labour, with tools like garden implements. This perfect apricot-skinned child emerged late, long nails, no hair and cloudy navy eyes that later turned black. A ravenous appetite. She arrived when demand feeding was not fashionable and a child in a hospital who was hungry every three hours rather than four was a nuisance. Later bouts of projectile vomiting exhausted us both. Poor Joseph. He became used to a daughter who would not fit into any prescribed formula – the proverbial round peg in a square hole.

'Could do better,' they said at school. Well of course she could but she had to enjoy her life and we always felt we should encourage but not force. And with the coming of hormones and the emergence of breasts came that streak of... oh, I coped with the purple hair at the family 'do', the talking behind backs, the snide remarks.

'And how are you doing in school now my dear? Veronica has been allowed to do four A levels a year early, such an industrious child, always working'.

'Her art results are excellent,' I spat.

'But that's not really a subject. Is it? What will she do in the future?'

What would she do indeed? We talked for nights, Joseph and I, and, as we walked around the park with the dogs, we agonised. What would she do? It had to be art college, but neither of us were happy, so many dangerous influences.

And, after two terms into college, it happened.

'It's my life,' she said. She sat opposite the fire with her green Oxfam coat pulled firmly round her young body, a wall of rebellious hostility. The coat was leather once. It had no buttons and it smelt like the animal it had been in its first life. Her legs were trousered in men's pyjamas tied at the ankles and those tiny size three feet rammed into huge Doc Martens.

'I'm not prepared to support people in your life apart from you,' Joseph said.

'It's my life,' she repeated, or rather, she screamed. 'It's my life and my friends. You have no right!'

She picked up a guitar, which she could not play, pulled on her brother's rucksack borrowed from his room, and ran into the night, the dark curls streaked with henna and dirt. We drove around the black roads, lamps lighting vacant shadows, desperate, frantic.

We found her at a friend's house. Her father handed her money.

'Don't sleep rough,' he pleaded. 'Let us know. Please let us know!'

When we returned, his voice sounded hollow, tired. We held each other. We wept for days.

'It's our turn to have big troubles. Everybody suffers big troubles in their marriage.'

For three weeks we heard nothing. We decided we had to try to enjoy the rest of what we had – another child, friends, a good life. We must put on a brave face, we decided.

'We'll go to Bath for the day,' Joseph said. He knew it was my favourite trip.

'A bit of lunch, a mooch round the antiques; scones for tea – it'll do us good.'

We walked around the streets of Bath on golden flagstones, elegant shops beckoning. But the spectre of that child walked beside us. On the icy ground, in the shadows of the cathedral, sat a dark-haired girl with a ragamuffin dog.

'Give us some change, Mister.'

He always gave money to the kids, but ten pounds? We looked at each other, sick hollows in our cheeks.

'This could be her,' he said. 'Where is she?'

How do you pretend? How do you keep your sanity? Eventually she rang.

'Darling, I love you,' I said. I wanted to say, 'I hate you for making your father look so grieved, so ashen' but I said only, 'Darling, I love you.'

She stayed away for five years. We don't really know what happened. But she phoned and we sent tickets and money and she came home from time to time, wanting hugs, smelling of another world, of damp rooms and raggedy clothes, which I tried to replace. Her face had lost its sparkle; it was deprived of passion, replaced by irritation. There were things we could never talk about, forbidden areas. If by chance we happened to brush by them in conversation, she would clamp her lips together. 'Don't want to talk about that,' she'd snap. And so to keep her feeling loved and wanted, I would hold the words and keep them unsaid. We would circumnavigate and then a few days later she would leave with the rucksack full of freshly cooked food and toiletries and a few small presents.

And then her beloved Grandpa fell ill, and she came home. Grandpa died two weeks later. After, at the family meal, Aunty Sophie took her hand.

'Get yourself a good strong man who will support you. At times like this you need a kind man. Someone who will really care. You never know when you will need someone.'

She said it was her Grandpa talking to her. She went away, finished the relationship and rang me, sobbing. 'Mum, it's over. I've finished it.'

'Darling, I'm so sorry,' I said, feeling such a hypocrite. 'Come home, my love – we love you. Come home.'

'But Mum, I've hurt you and Dad so much.'

'Darling, Don't worry. Come home. It's over. It's forgotten.'

I put the phone down and knocked on the kitchen window. Joseph was attending to his kidney bean plants and the fragrant sweet peas he always grew just for me. He was totally engrossed. Men are so fortunate. I'm such a typical woman. Family concerns are always uppermost in my head. We clung to each other shaking with the idea that we might be lucky enough to get our daughter back. Afraid that if we so much as spoke, it would crumble, tumble like the clematis seeds that floated around our summer garden. But that was past. My daughter was returning. The day she did, we made a bonfire of her old clothes at the bottom of the garden – a strange woolly epitaph to a time we preferred to forget. And a month later, we took her to London. We waved her off at the airport, for a group holiday – a white-faced, withdrawn individual, with a bag of new clothes and a sliver of hope between us. When she returned, the giggle came with her. Her face was glowing. The grey pallor which had dressed her body had been sloughed like a discarded snakeskin. She had swum and hiked. She had laughed, sat by campfires and sung, found new friends in another town. There were years to make up, aeons to enjoy. Her father began to laugh again; started to work in his office with the faint sound of classical music from a radio and a window open to let in the summer sunshine.

Just a few months later, she decided to move again but now it was different. Her new friends had persuaded her to join them. Each time she called home she was breathless with excitement. There was a party. A crowd were going out for a meal. It was going to be a bit expensive but... *Go*, we said. *Enjoy, live your life, have fun.* She now had a job, badly paid but respectable, and Joseph gladly paid for extras, new shoes, a jacket, tickets. At last we were a family again, not always physically together, but considering and caring.

Time passed. We had now developed a rather enjoyable routine, my daughter and I. Maybe three times a year I would visit. We would do a gallery, have coffee and then a little lunch, nothing too expensive. Then we would wander round a few ooh-ahh shops, Fortnums or Harrods, buy some very small presents, a new lipstick, a fat new paperback, chocolates to take home and then I would return on the train. But then:

'There's someone I'd like you to meet, Mum.'

Already seated in the coffee shop was a young man, freshly shaven, sparkling eyes, in a suit. They exchanged looks, my baby and this man, as Joseph and I had done so many years ago. They were holding the details of flats – estate agents' printouts. Although they were sitting with me, they saw only each other.

Margaret and I sit in the kitchen. The clock ticks rhythmically and we can still hear the faint barking of dogs. I've made an effort today: homemade tomato and basil soup, couscous with mint from the garden – fresh, fragrant tips. There is a salad loaded with rich puy lentils, chick peas, carrots and hummus and a whole olive bread made that morning. I hug her after my proud announcement.

Margaret puts her capable knitter's arms around my neck and hugs me back with gusto. 'Wonderful news, love. I'm so pleased.'

She's with me in my happiness, my best friend. We remember a golden day we spent many years past when the children were tiny, two families, raspberry picking beside a sunlit cornfield.

'You can play close by,' we said. 'Stay by the swings and slides but don't go into the cornfield, because it belongs to the farmer and he'll be cross.' The adults became absorbed in the picking, fingers plucking firm warm clusters of berries, tumbling into baskets. Then a laugh distracted us. There in the silken waving movement of the cornfield walked five very small heads in slow procession – the temptation had been too much. In that moment, we shared everything:

41

the continual conflict of creating a perfect childhood for our children – they looked so beautiful doing wrong – and at the same time, establishing discipline. We mirrored each other's emotions.

*   *   *

The hall was magnificently decorated with cream and red roses. People enjoyed themselves. Some who knew us very well indulged in the luxury of a small tear, but this was a happy occasion. The cake stood proud in the foyer resplendent with fondant icing teddies and silver hearts and stars and my baby stood next to her new husband, a beautiful woman in ivory silk with sparkling tiara and veil.

THE TEMPTATION OF SILK

It was just another Monday. An overcast day. No wind to speak of. Black clouds merging into a leaden sky, and a forecast of continuous rain for the week. Selwyn Isaac Shackleton Yarrow dawdled down the High Street Arcade on his way to the gentleman's outfitters where he had worked for twenty three years. But a Coke-can rattling on a tinny axis caught his foot and stopped him. He caught his reflection in the lingerie shop window and began staring, then pursed his lips. He pinched his cheekbones, watching the colour rise above the faintest shadow, and continued gazing.

Why, on that day, did he suddenly abandon his past inhibitions and look? After all this time! Were they watching him inside the shop? Would they talk if he...? His mind was filled with temptation. Butterfly thoughts. *Supposing... maybe I could... perhaps... I could say that I wanted something for my sister.* Never before had he had the courage to steal even a glance. *Oh dear Lord.*

What would my mother...? Still he hesitated, hovering like an insect near a perfumed flower. Eventually, scanning his watch, he extricated himself from the view and made his way to work.

But in those few seconds, in front of the shop window, while breaking the tramlines of his routine, Selwyn had tasted rebellion, fragrant with adrenaline.

The heavy mahogany door clunked a familiar noise as the brass lock fell back on the receiver. 'Morning, Mr Jeffries,' he called. He went through to the staff room, and hung his camel wool coat carefully on one of the better wooden hangers, smoothing away imaginary creases. Then he laid his brief case on one of the wooden chairs, and took out spray bathroom cleaner and a clean J-cloth wrapped in a polythene bag. He scrubbed the blue Formica next to the kettle. When he had decided that all dirt traces had been removed, he laid a crisp linen napkin on the space, then took out a bone-china cup, saucer and plate, also from his briefcase, together with his foil-wrapped, poached chicken breast sandwiches. Finally, he added a small silver-plated knife and a carefully rolled Western Mail to the arrangement. Then, readjusting his clothing, he took a deep breath and strode onto the sales floor.

Today's customers were easy. Mr Hopkins for another grey flannel sports-jacket identical to last year's version, with a need to move slightly the button pulling over the stomach. Mr Hopkins laughed, patting the offending paunch and saying, 'A combination of too much married life, my man, and an overindulgence in pudding, port and Stilton at Christmas.' For seconds Selwyn mused how 'married life' put on the pounds, but was too interested in his own concerns that day to give the thought more than glancing consideration. A married lady needing a tie for her husband's birthday was his next customer. What a choice, he'll be back in changing that next week, he thought, as he gift-wrapped the purple shot with orange silk. One of the buyer's mistakes. After a beige knitted cardigan trimmed with suede, it was lunch-time. Usually, he took his meal on his own in the small staff room with Radio Four playing quietly in the background. But today he had to get out of the shop. He repacked his sandwiches, serviette, Western Mail, while downing a double strength coffee, drunk with a shudder, and eyeballs raised to heaven. Oh, the courage of caffeine! Then with moist plump hands pushed firmly into yellow Gucci gloves, he strode out of the shop. It felt colder. The lunch-time air was dipped in frost. A tired time, pushing into February, when the remnants of the January sales would fight for space with the mass of boxes delivered with the new spring range. Soon it would be Easter. He would be expected home. His mother would pick out her best black from the depths of a camphor-soaked mothballed wardrobe. It seemed to contain nothing but black – pleats, tucks of prickly wool, barathea and her only piece of jewellery: a mourning ring with a small lock of his father's hair snipped from his head with embroidery scissors, as he lay staring into nothing. She would be on the phone any day now, urging him to remember his piety, atone for his sins, insisting that he helped her arrange the church flowers. Stiff, waxy, Madonna lilies. Chrysanthemums, jasmine and ivy. A sickly odour that caught in his throat, reminding him of his father's passing. He heard the voices. *Now is the moment. Take your chance – before it's too late.*

Almost without thinking, he made his way back to the arcade. Was that the brush of vast angel wings about his body? He was at the lingerie shop window. He examined his reflection again and felt colour run from his neck up the sides of his ears, until his face had reddened like a fat turkey for slaughter.

Selwyn, you're guilty about something, aren't you? I can always tell.

He ignored the voice. Next year he would be forty: too late – too old. But his feet seemed glued to the pavement. He looked down at the carefully polished brogues – *Don't miss the piece underneath, next to the sole. Only people of true breeding polish that part. It always shows.*

He was back in his bedroom staring at that vision of hell his mother had placed opposite his bed the day he was born. Hieronymus Bosch. He had grown up with the fear of demons, goblins and monsters consuming his body parts. As a toddler, he'd cower under the covers, terrified, asking Jesus for forgiveness, and his mother Edna would hug him, forcing him out of bed onto on his knees, revelling in his repentance.

Then at five he joined Abermorlais local primary and a new torture began.

'Your whole name boy... All your other names as well... Come on hurry up... We haven't got all day,' muttered Mr Morrison, known as Chalky the Death because of his skeletal looks.

Selwyn whispered his first name under his breath. Then out gushed the others in one nervous chain. 'Selwyn, Isaac' – in memory of his grandfather – 'Shackleton' – after his father's hero – 'Yarrow.'

'Selwyn, Isaac, Shackleton, Yarrow.' The children sang it as they circled the playground – a tarmac piece surrounded by stone walls to keep the children in and the sheep out.

'Selwyn, Isaac, Shackleton, Yarrow'. The girls sang it as they jumped between skipping ropes, and sang it sitting on the school wall, legs swinging as they wove and passed cats-cradles. And the boys sang it in between kicking the ball between two piles of coats stacked into a makeshift goal. An older brother of one of the boys heard his sibling mutter the string of names, and put Selwyn's initials together.

'Well good Lord! The poor lad's called Sissy all bar the one s.'

From that day, Selwyn's name turned into a rhyme.

'Selwyn Isaac, Shackleton Yarrow,
Slipped down the mountain on his father's barrow,
Slipped down the mountain, fell on his bum,
Selwyn Isaac's a sissy,
And his mother is glum.'

So Selwyn obtained his badge of difference, that would set him apart from the others for the rest of his school life. It would stain his future like the inky black index finger his mother would scrub with carbolic every day after school.

Selwyn shuddered. His school days enveloped him like a chalky phantom. But now was his chance. It had to be now. He'd left his mother in Merthyr. He'd made a new life for himself. He had to make a stand – show her, before she died.

He looked down at his watch. He had been standing at the window for a quarter of an hour now, and thought of the staff inside watching him. *I suppose* he considered, *in that sort of shop they're used to men hovering outside. But, dear Lord, for their wives or mistresses'* He felt the heat about his face pass to his belly and lower torso and, despite the weather, a small trickle of perspiration ran down his back.

'Now or never, Selwyn,' he muttered. He pushed open the door – there was a fragrance of flowers. A tall vase of freesias and carnations reached towards the ceiling, tented with gold lamé and, on the side wall next to the stairs, a large mirror watched and judged his every move.

'Can I help you, sir?' said a greying lady behind a counter festooned with small coloured items of lingerie.

His mouth was dry. For seconds he was speechless. He licked the edges of his lips and dragged a parched tongue over his teeth. 'I... I... would like to see... '

'Yes, sir... ' She looked back at him. It was a kindly face.

'I've never... '

'No, sir... something for a wife... a girlfriend perhaps?'

'No, may I see some... ' He looked around for ideas, staring at the stands arranged with nightdresses, bras...

'Some petticoats?'

'Er... '

'Full length or just half-length?' She hesitated, seeing his confusion, before saying clearly, 'Would you like to see some petticoats with the bust included or just from the waist down?'

'Maybe just a half to start.'

She began to open wooden drawers, pulling out pinks, reds, blues, creams, blacks, in exquisite fabrics – silks, tulles and satins and...

'This is our best seller, sir,' she said proudly. 'Oyster satin silk – from China. The lady who owns the shop makes these herself... look, French seams double stitched... coffee lace trim... Look at the sheen, feel the fabric... gorgeous.'

Selwyn moved fingers forward, fighting a sense of sublime catatonic pleasure, and smoothed the silk, feeling it kiss his fingertips.

'It is beautiful,' he murmured.

'What size, sir?'

'Oh I don't know. Large I would think. And longish?'

'Yes, sir. A long length – that's very popular – unless she's tiny.'

'No, no. A large, long length would be wonderful.'

She carefully wrapped the petticoat in pink tissue paper and placed the parcel in a black plastic bag with the name of the shop, *Moonlight*, on the outside, next to the logo of a lady in a state of undress, in gold.

'Do you think I could possibly have a plain bag... I have to go back to the office?' He managed to utter the few words while his body remained in a state of ecstatic elevation.

She winked. She winked at him! He was sure it was a wink. He walked out of the shop with a plain black carrier ignoring his mother's demons. He was in a state of bliss.

Walking home, he knew his life would start from now.

He let himself into his Pontcanna flat. He smoothed the cat, luxuriating in the responsive purr. He put food in the bowl, washed his hands and then, after unwrapping a new Carmina Burana CD, slid the rainbow disk deftly into its cavity. He turned up the volume to disrespectful. Then he walked into the bathroom, ran a bath and lit all the elegant church candles he'd arranged around the edge. Finally he removed every item of clothing and peeled the oyster–silk petticoat out of its bag. He lay it reverently on the bed. Somewhere in the background the telephone rang, intermittently.

It rang in his head. But it was ignored, along with the scream of demons, the vision of gilded phosphorescence, and the beat of heavy white wings.

A PIECE OF SKY

'Blast, blast, damn and blast. I wish she didn't have to bloody dust all the time. I swear she hides the bits of jigsaw just to give me aggravation!'

Jacob Pengelly pushed his tired captain's cap back on his head and then readjusted it forward. Some of his grey hair became caught under the sweatband and stuck out from his reddened neck like dirty seagull's feathers. He deliberately scraped his chair on the bare lino so that the scream echoed through the house.

'Couldn't the damn woman have left things alone?' he cried.

He looked through the window at the darkening light and heard the sea crashing on the rocks.

'She'll be back in a minute and our peace will be shattered by her bloody twittering.'

Jacob looked at his dogs, Nelson at his feet and Pirate feigning sleep on the couch, on his back, legs akimbo, one eye open.

'The boss will be back soon. She won't put up with us in here together. She won't stand for that malarkey a minute.'

He rose slowly, flexing rigid limbs. At once the two black collies were at the French windows, panting and wagging their tails. Jacob pushed the door and the dogs ran out in a cacophony of barking. The dusk was moving fast into night and a woolly mist smothered the edge of the sea and sky like an old grey sailor's blanket.

'Come on, lads. Let's get the weather while there's still time. In a minute she'll be back with half the bloody supermarket, and me and you will be banished to the kitchen.'

Jacob waved his stick at the rocks as the glass door slammed behind him. She'd only fuss if he went the cliff-side way. But the Pengellys had always lived with the taste of the sea and its rocks in their bellies. He was proud of his family tradition. Some of the Pengellys went back hundreds of years. They had smuggling blood in their veins. It was a respected profession in the past – raised the standard of the humble fisherman – and brought employment and prosperity to the bay. The wind shrieked around Jacob's body and knives of cold stabbed through his thin blazer to his aching bones.

'Too late for the bloody coat now,' he muttered.

The sea was a hungry beast clawing at the tiny cottages knotted around Pengelly Hall – Jacob's home. He fought the buffets of the wind feeling his way down the narrow-cut slippery steps chiselled out of black rock. He rested on a flattened edge that led to one of the myriads of secret caves, their purpose ended. He liked to stop there and turn. He always left the lights on in the house and, when he shifted stiffly to face his home with the anger of the sea behind him, the face of Pengelly Hall shone out like a lightship. His cloudy-blue eyes misted over with pride.

'It's bloody wonderful – that sight – isn't it, boys? You could pull a few ships in with that show.'

Jacob rubbed his eyes with his blazered sleeve, trumpeted a blow with a frayed red kerchief and stumbled down the few last steps till the smack of the sea and chains of spray were so close they seemed to taunt his gaunt frame.

Why don't my boys love this place? he thought. *Can't they feel it?* His sons had never tasted the special magic. He ran his fingers over jagged rocks wet with brine that held the ghosts – his ancestors' bodies and the spirits of the village lads smashed in their efforts to plunder barrels of whisky and brandy, silks and spices.

Jacob turned around, called the dogs and limped back up the dark cliff-side. His heart was banging in his chest.

'Bloody sciatica, pulling pain.' He rubbed his sides. 'If Doctor Lennard and the boys had their way, I'd be in hospital now having two iron hips fitted about me backside, and you two lads in a home!' At last he reached the top. He walked over lawns ankle-deep in mist and just as he had the house in full sight, the windows cut out one by one, enveloping him in darkness. The dogs barked.

'Damn and blast. She's back, that's the end of our peace. Into the back kitchen with the lot of us. We have all that space, and we have to live in that bloody back room falling over each other.'

Jacob knew that the French windows would now be locked. He pulled his cap over his eyes and breathed deeply to assume an assertive pose, and made his best effort to stride around the darkened path made slimy by the constant rain and wind. It was lucky he could see the collar of white fur around the dogs' necks and the tips of their tails wagging white in the gloom. Past the bins and the coal house, Jacob arrived at the door to the back kitchen and winced, waiting for the rail of complaints.

'I suppose you've been down the cliff again with your bad hips?' Millicent chided.

'Yes, I bloody have. We're in for a few days of rough,' said Jacob, rubbing reddened hands channelled with thick bluish-purple veins.

'But it's so dangerous!'

'Woman, I'm used to it!'

Jacob watched Millicent emptying a small packet of lentils, some barley, a pound of granulated sugar, economy tea bags and a pound of self-raising flour out of a plastic bag into a faded cupboard which must have had a coating of eau-de-nil paint many years ago. A scowl set on his mouth.

'Do we really need all that stuff?'

Millicent turned her back on Jacob, pretending to ignore his words. Then she pulled her wiry body out of the cupboard, stood up and faced him, hands on hips, her thin face red with effort.

'I know,' she retorted. 'Evie could make a small tin of sardines go round you and the two boys and have plenty left for the next day. But I'm not Evie. I'm

Millicent. Surely you can tell the difference by now! Good Lord, Jacob. It's been fifteen years.'

Jacob's sides ached. He turned in temper and picked up a cracked cup that sat draining next to the sink and threw it in Millicent's direction. It smashed close to the remaining bag of shopping.

Millicent picked up the pieces of crockery, dropped them in a cracked plastic bucket under the sink, emptied the bag onto the kitchen table and turned to confront Jacob.

'Look Jacob. It's not that much.'

On the worn wood lay a packet of cheese, a sliced loaf of bread, a few tins of beans and pilchards, some cleaning fluids, an economy packet of toilet rolls and a small bottle of cooking sherry.

'We are managing on nothing, absolutely nothing.'

Jacob grunted. He had regretted his temper straight away. She wasn't such a bad old thing. He could remember that gap when Evie was gone and life was a blur of empty rum bottles and mouldy loaves. But the words were buried fathoms deep.

'I'm, I'm...'

He walked over to his chair and sat staring out through the black glass and beyond. His mind journeyed to far-off waters, seas crawling with serpents and shipwrecks crashing into matchsticks. He missed that world. Millicent was hovering near him. Damn it. He should talk to her. They were in for a few bad days and there was only his jigsaw and the Shipping Forecast to pass the time. But the words stayed trapped. Anyway, any minute he would hear the announcer – 'This is the BBC... ' It would speak the mantra of German Bight and Heligoland and he would be at his bridge, dynamic, important, waiting for guidance to steer his lads through the slap of the waves, to safety.

Now they were rigid – his waves – trapped in jigsaws. He had an order in the village shop for maritime jigsaws – the bigger the better. Five thousand pieces with masts, and rigging and spinnaker. Sometimes, when the mood was good, he would get lost inside the picture. Feel the sails slap against the wind, hear the cries of the boys – most of them gone now.

'Jacob, Jacob, pilchard and potatoes?'

'Yes yes,' said Jacob, 'that's fine. You can't beat a good tin of pilchards.' His voice softened slightly. He switched on the radio and Millicent sniffed, noticing the change in his voice.

'Rum...?' she said But the south-easterlies had swallowed his consciousness. She poured a small tot of rum and set it next to the jigsaw. He drank without acknowledgement.

'Jacob. We have to talk. We don't have enough for the bills. We need... we live in this vast house. I know the house is ours, but there's council tax, water, electric, phone... although we don't use it really... and we have to have a little food... I'm not managing!'

But Jacob was with the waves.

'I'm going to get work. There's not much I can do at my age, but they said in the village there's a couple of fishing smacks that pay for lugworm for bait. I'm going digging in the estuary. It's only a few pounds but... Jacob, Jacob, do you hear? I'm going to do some digging. We have to get some cash and I know you won't ask the boys.'

'Ask the boys? Ask the boys what?'

Millicent sank into the chair. It was hopeless. She pulled at her tapestry, which she had bought in a charity shop after Jacob complained about the noise of the knitting needles.

'Clatter, clatter, sounds like bloody witches' teeth. Can't you stop that bloody racket?'

*   *   *

Early the next morning, Jacob reached out to the side of the bed and an empty space.

Where was the blasted woman now? Painfully, he pulled himself from a mound of grey blankets and felt the shiver of the morning light; his bony, calloused feet tentatively touched the frozen lino. The two dogs sat wagging on the landing.

'Where's she gone, boys?'

He made his way down to the kitchen, the draughts piercing his frayed long-johns. On the table lay a packet of instant porridge, a cracked pottery bowl, a spoon and a note written on the back of an old Christmas card.

'Jacob. I'm out digging lugworm. See you later.'

Jacob scratched his head. 'Why? Why was she digging for lugworm?'

He boiled the kettle, mixed a full bowl of instant porridge for the dogs and a large portion for himself. Flakes of porridge floated across the floor and over the table.

'Shipping Forecast in a second and then back to the jigsaw.'

Jacob dragged on a pair of jeans that had been hanging over the bar of the Aga and a clean Guernsey left drying. Then he put his bowl, together with the dogs' bowl, into the sink and returned to his jigsaw.

Time must have passed. Was he asleep? He could hear the moan of the sea with a million drowning voices and the wind tasting whitened tree roots and flinging boulders like coppers into the sucking surf.

Blast it, he thought. She said something about the windows. The boys were always fussing about the windows. We can stuff the cracks with bits of blanket. I'll tell her when she comes back.

He gazed down in satisfaction, his jigsaw completed. No, damn it, there was a piece missing. A piece of sky. He looked around. Checked the floor below him. Pulled back his cap and scratched his head – perplexed. Then he returned the cap. His face darkened into a purple tempest. 'Bloody woman with all her cleaning! Just one bloody piece of sky. Is there any point? I can never finish... '

The phone rang, jarring his consciousness, and he looked vaguely in its direction. But he ignored its persistent ring. His body shook with involuntary shudders. 'Come on boys. We're going out.'

He opened the French windows and the wind pulled at the flimsy glass but he never heard the crash. Jacob hesitated for a few minutes then drew himself up into his officer's stance.

'Not down, lads, but up onto the higher cliffs along the path.'

At the very top, chest tight with exertion, he stood stooped and tired. He reached down to touch his dogs at the side of his body and noticed his slippered feet. The hungry wind knifed through his body. Although it was mid-morning, the sky was dark and the sea churned below him impatient and needy.

Seagulls called with human cries as they swooped and soared the currents. Suddenly, the pain was gone. He felt strength and watched as the images of his seaman days flooded his mind.

'I cannot leave this place,' he said.

*   *   *

The next morning they found Jacob Pengelly. He was wearing his captain's cap, jeans and a Guernsey, slippers, a flimsy blazer and in its side pocket was a small piece of jigsaw – a piece of sky.

STEALING BABY

'Doctor will be here in a moment to look at those arms, so you'd best have a wash and make yourself tidy.'

Was that a smear of sympathy in her voice? They call my cell 'the coffin'. It dosses in the corner of the basement set aside from the others, in the old part of the prison. It's painted a muddy pink – like the dead blancmange they serve in this place, although gashes of blue and yellow burst through where it's worn. The narrow bed with its worn-out green blanket skulks along the wall like a wounded dog. On the opposite side are a stainless steel toilet and a small wooden table and chair.

Oh yes. They're very good. They allow me mags and a radio and a bit of makeup. I did have a poster of Brad Pitt, but one of the girls trashed it along with my jeans and my Stereophonics T-shirt and I've been in solitary ever since. The other girls hated me when they found out what I'd done. But I told them I would never hurt a child. I wanted to love it. I longed for that tight pink fist clutching my finger and the soft downy head nuzzling my bare skin. I still don't understand... I've always wanted one.

I used to imagine pushing a pram with my own child snuggled safely in fleecy blankets like a new apricot tucked in a basket. I'd lift it out of its warmth to feed it. A new needy sucking thing, with velvety skin close to my neck, and a warm scent fresh like digestive biscuits.

Years ago I said to my mother, 'When I'm older, I'm going to have a baby.' She choked on her tea as if it was a great joke and, in a hoity-toity voice, she answered:

'Have a baby. You couldn't make the gravy...'

I never really followed the connection but I knew at the back of her mind she was thinking of Toby's death. She never forgave me for it.

*　　　　*　　　　*

He arrived on December 24th early in the morning and everyone was very excited. They all said how wonderful it was that there was a boy in the family at last and the telephone rang and flowers arrived in big, big bunches and Mummy and Daddy had loads of post.

They forgot to decorate the tree. I'd waited for weeks. Mummy always decorated it with me. We'd pull out the box from the big white cupboard at the top of the house. It would smell of dust and sometimes there would be spiders inside. But I couldn't wait to see the golden soldiers and the tiny, red-carved elephants that Grandad brought back from India, and the angel with the shimmery, silvery wings that always fell down once. There would be parcels underneath. I wanted a baby doll with real hair and a dummy and all the clothes and a toy buggy – I'd seen it in the shop, and maybe some roller-skates.

I was allowed to see Toby three hours after he was born. Daddy said to be very quiet and gentle and, after my supper and my bath, he led me into their bedroom. Mummy lay in the big bed. Her face was as white as the moon and her hair was loose and floated over the pillow like a mermaid in the water. In her arms was a tiny baby wrapped in a blue blanket. His face was red, crumpled with bluish lips and he was crying, but Mummy kept kissing him and saying how special he was and how we had to be grateful that the good Lord had sent him. Then the baby started to scream like the cat when he squashed his tail. I didn't like the noise and I wanted to push him back inside Mummy's tummy. I wanted to be in the big bed with Mummy, not that special boy.

For days and days Mummy stayed in the room and the doctor came and Daddy said that she had been very poorly and we must whisper all the time and I must not play with my xylophone or trumpet.

I didn't mean to wake her.

Then they said I was a big girl, and it was time for me to start school. We went to a special shop and bought a blue cardboardy hat, a blue striped dress and a brown, stiff satchel. My teacher was very nice. Her name was Mrs Wilson. She wore big jumpers with belts pulled around her middle and her hair was grey like the knitted wire stuff we use to clean the pots and pans. She taught me ABCs and painting and numbers, and in the afternoon she told us stories. But I didn't like school and I didn't like the milk. They should have given it to the baby boy in my house. I wanted to be home with my pussy-cat and Mummy and Daddy and have cuddles in the big bed.

Then one afternoon, Mummy wanted to sleep and she told me to watch Toby. He was in his carry-cot in the sitting room. His face was pink instead of red and he was wearing a small white hat with a yellow teddy on the top and a yellow baby-gro. He started to cry. Funny quiet grizzles at the beginning. I did watch him. I told them... the cat. They said I should have called them. But the noises stopped and they both looked so comfy squeezed in together. Toby must have been happy, because he'd stopped crying.

*   *   *

They are very kind to me here but I don't like the food and I don't like the milk. Leanne my friend had a baby. She told me that Carl said it would be alright for them to do it because nothing happened the first time especially if you stood up. She said she felt OK after – that it wasn't that special. Just a bit of heaving and grunting and then it was all over. She was often late so she didn't worry. When her belly started to grow we went to Boots together and bought one of those tests and it was too late. She was afraid to tell her mum but eventually she did. There were terrible rows and her mum screamed and her dad muttered behind his Echo about her being the same as all the rest, and said that Carl had to marry her. But he'd done a runner.

So after the baby was born, I went to visit Leanne in hospital. She asked me if I wanted to see her. They'd taken the baby down to the nursery to give Leanne some sleep. There were rows of babies in plastic cots.

Each had a teddy or a furry bunny at the end of the cot and had funny knitted hats tied around their heads in bright pink, orange and green. Leanne's eyes were red with crying, and she kept saying how she didn't want to look after a child and how her mother said she'd never be able to go out clubbing again. As soon as I saw that tiny creature, I wanted it. I wanted the baby in the cot. I was doing her a favour.

I planned it like they do in the films. It was easy. The next time I visited, I put a nightie, dressing-gown and some slippers in my Nike rucksack. And after the visit, I popped into the Ladies and changed. Leanne had told me the security number so I could visit more. I just walked into the nursery. The nurses were busy in the little side wards at the far end, with the prem. babies. I looked about. Then leaned over and took Leanne's baby. She cuddled close into my shoulder making snuffly noises. So I knew she really liked me. But as I walked down Somerset Road, I heard some shouting and a man in a brown coat, the hospital porter, I think, moved near me. People were staring. Then a policewoman came towards me talking in a low voice. She was smiling at me. She understood that I needed the baby. Then she pulled it out of my arms and the man in the brown coat pushed me away from the child and I fell on the ground. The baby started to cry, and the rain sharpened to hail. Ice crystals spat on my body. I'd cut myself badly. There was blood from my elbows and my knees. Then into a car. Strong lights in my eyes. My fingers rolled in black sticky stuff and squeezed tight over paper. The flash of photographs, this side, that side. They emptied my pockets and pushed me into a cell. They never gave me a chance to say goodbye to my baby.

I was going to call her Cherise. I'd made it up myself. She was a beautiful little girl with the tiniest pink fingers, like the petals of a flower, and blonde fluffy hair sticking out on top like a baby bird in a nest. I would never have hurt her. I would have loved her. Dressed her up in my doll's clothes and pushed her in my doll's pram.

The food in here is strange. I don't like the milk...

My mother never visits. Sometimes I get a small letter on lilac paper. It usually says 'Thinking of you. Your Mother.' But there are never any kisses.

Now I stare through the bars at my patch of sky and wonder when it's hot and when it's cold. The rooms are sealed – the temperatures managed by switches and plugs. I can just remember the blow of the wind down the Mall. Inside-out umbrellas like dead crows in the gutter with wings up-tilted lying next to last night's party junk.

A visitor came to see me. I said I didn't mind. She said I could talk about anything. She told me to spill out my thoughts and she would help me. I expect she meant well. She was dressed like my Aunty Mildred in large flowing linen trousers and a cream coat down to her ankles, and masses of coloured beads. She looked as if she wanted to be in a foreign film. I think she hoped that Lawrence of Arabia would whisk her away from her blue dralon rooms with matching budgie, and cottage suite with its smell of boiled eggs and soldiers, and her classic films in the afternoons. But he never did. I know she meant well but she seemed so relieved when they called that time was up. She never came again.

The doctor comes regularly and looks at my arms and now they don't allow me any knives for food and the nurse has to cut my nails. They keep asking me why I cut, when they change the dressings. I know I'd been feeling low. The square of trapped light was grey in my window and I had this pain. Mum had sent one of her lilac notes... it smelt of her. The pain started to thrum through my ears as my heart beat faster and faster. My hands felt wet. I kept rubbing them against my trousers. The blood was red in my eyes and I kept seeing Toby sleeping in the cot. He was just sleeping. I'd been OK, and then that note. And the perfume... I smelt her hate. I needed to slice the pain out of my body. Dig the bad out of my body. I was holding Cherise... my baby... then the blood was running over my arm down onto the floor.

*   *   *

Doctor's been. He had a present for me. A baby doll with real hair and a cot. I can change her clothes and feed her when I want and her face, hands and feet are the softest pink and she cries 'Mama' to me.

GRANDMOTHER TO A HEARTBEAT

It's a sleepy Saturday afternoon interrupted by a bright tap-tapping on the porch door. I move quickly, anxious, wiping hands on my apron. Their faces are squashed cartoon-like against the glass. Why didn't they use the bell?

'We've got news!' she cries.

My baby, now thirty years old, dances into the hallway wearing her father's seventies flared jeans commandeered months ago. Some of her long, sloe black curls are pulled into a purple velvet scrunchy but strands fall over her shoulders, bouncing with excitement. Her face glows with a new joy and David looks at her with devoted pride.

'You're pregnant, aren't you?' I choke. A secret box is prized open within me: an unknown place that spills a kaleidoscope of emotions. I look at my daughter and son-in-law, their unlined faces so positive, so beautiful.

'Can we wake up Dad? I know he's been low but he won't mind for that, will he?' She pulls a small frown.

'Darlings, how could he possibly mind?' I respond, hugging them both in a giant cuddle, tasting their joy, relishing my own.

As I run up the stairs to call my husband, the full impact of the news has not completely filtered into my mind. I push open the door with a creak. 'Love?' He wakes instantly – it's a light afternoon rest. The room is cool and the soft filmy curtains blow a summer curtsy to the open window.

'What's up? Everything OK?' He sits up with a start as if shocked.

I perch on the edge of the bed and take his outstretched hand to calm him. 'Nothing to worry about. Darling, the kids are here. They've got a bit of news.'

He looks at my expression. Although I am smiling, I know it's a twisted quirky thing and the tears roll – I've never been very good at the tight upper lip.

'She's...!'

I nod with an emphatic move of my head, incapacitated by the tears, the flood of emotion. A quick movement and he's out of bed. We embrace – a closeness of body and limbs and a familiarity bred out of thirty-three years. In seconds he is dressed. We go downstairs and he opens a bottle for everyone except my baby to share and we make jokes about aiming on sticks with blue markers and pour cups of thick Welsh tea with slices of sweet and sharp homemade lemon cake. Our rescue collie barks with the family's excitement and tries to steal everybody's portion. And

I watch. I see the two young heads: ecstatic faces close, drinking and kissing, and the older grey head happy but restrained by the anxieties of experience.

Later, in the privacy of our own room, where the cool sheets whisper intimacy, I slip over to his side. We embrace. I nestle my head into the crook of his shoulder and slide my arm around his waist. His voice is still a little choked.

'So what do you think then, Grandma? A bit of news, eh!'

As we talk, pictures flash through my mind. Her agonising birth – a three-day labour with a child finally prised from a reluctant womb with metal instruments. A perfect, minuscule infant in a hospital cot, starving always starving, sucking from a sore breast, and a tearful, exhausted mother terrified at the responsibility of this screaming conglomeration of wriggling arms, legs and voice.

'Just a bit of colic, dear. She'll settle down. Give it time.'

And then hollow-eyed nights and nights of pacing and rocking in return for another change of clothes and gratitude for a burp. The school years of ballet practice, swimming club: *What kind of sandwiches do you want...? Could do better*, and *that's not fair, everybody else is having... going.*

Will she be all right? Will she cope? Will they manage?

Days pass. It is Friday and she is coming to help me bake. We have always enjoyed the process of baking together, since she was a tiny child. We baked her wedding cake, mixing and laughing at my maths that produced double the amount of cake needed and stirring in wishes, spices, almonds, brandy and yet more brandy. That was a good cake. That was a good time. It's an excuse for her to come around, a chance to talk: to share familiarity sourced out of a basic, old-fashioned process. I like to make fresh for the weekend. A batch of soft white bread, worked and shaped, with a hint of saffron, gilded with egg yolk sprinkled with poppy seeds, and a mango cake: one for her, one for us. Mango cake is only made in our family for special occasions, as it is expensive. It needs the flesh of two ripe mangos, processed with the juice and rind of two sharp juicy lemons. It was my late father-in-law's favourite and it seems appropriate to include him in the celebrations. The kitchen feels warm and welcoming with a buttery scent from lunch-time's toast. I light the gas. We get out the flour and soft margarine and lay them on the kitchen top with eggs and the mangos. She offers to peel them and soon leaves a pile of flesh for me, and the stones to suck for her. As we sieve the flour and cream the sugar with the marg', we talk about the future little one and she asks if we will all bake together?

'Yes,' I say, 'of course,' delighted to think that I have created a tradition that came from my late mother and hopefully will continue into the future. But seedling feelings are stirring within me, and some are unwelcome. In an area of my mind where worries needle into soft sensitive places, I see myself as Whistler's mother in the Musée D'Orsay in Paris, mouth fixed in a tight grimace, back straight, small white lace cap sitting rigid in a hard wooden chair. She doesn't realise that by announcing her news she has changed my personal status. Some of my friends have viewed the impending 'grandship' with horror. But I am not like them. The voice of reason returns. This is the grandchild you have dreamt of. This is what you have always wanted. When all the cakes and bread lie cooling on the silver racks, David calls for her and after more tea they leave.

Now the house is quiet, I decide to have a bath. We worked hard in the past, Joseph and I, crazy hours, he prescribing glasses and revamping, selling and letting old buildings, me catering for weddings, dinner parties, sewing shirts, lingerie, even dog beds, and now we are enjoying the rewards – a new bathroom constructed out of a neglected part of the back of the house. Cream beige and white tiles reminiscent of cararra marble that sing of hot piazzas, an off-white bath with chrome and gold fittings and soft, velvety, lilac towels. The water runs warm, a soothing pouring sound. I add a little rose and jojoba essence which floats on the top in golden beads and I put on some classical stuff – the Bruch violin concerto. The gentle second movement always prickles the hairs on the back of my neck and sometimes produces tears.

I take my clothes off quickly, not looking at my body and climb in, sitting snug against the back. Then I pull my knees towards me, with my hands clasped, not allowing the water to enter me – and I fold my head and my body forward into a foetal position, tight. Gradually, the warmth, the perfume and the music filter through the membrane of my fears and the tension percolates out. I begin to straighten, then stretch, my torso and my legs. Eventually I lie back, relax, and contemplate the body in front of me. It's not done very often but seems necessary to reflect at personally meaningful times: a kind of revision of life.

Sometimes it is kinder to look in the bath than the mirror – something to do with standing and the pull of gravity. Out of the water my flesh makes downward inclinations, whereas a semi-floating position restores it. My breasts float up to the surface tipped with good nipples – at least they're still the same. My stomach is flatter – the water helps me to pull it in. Yes, I do try to watch it, the weight, most of the time, except when custard calls. It's that comforting warm creaminess... sad girl; I make it out of Soya milk and sweeteners but still with good old Birds. And on a Saturday night if we are not going out. Everybody has to have one vice don't they? And the thighs and legs? Well, in the hot water, lying down, the cellulite magically disappears and I can't see the varicose vein operation scars.

My eyes glance from my body to a more comfortable scrutinising area – out of the top windows, which are not frosted, and to the sky. A skein of cirrus casts its milky floating filaments across a perfect blue. I can hear the buzz of next door's lawnmower mingling with the cries of children playing – neighbours' grandchildren. Framed by the glass, the beech trees move gently. Their limbs are heavy with summer green and the fuzzy, woven circle of a nest sits balanced at a rustic angle – like a leafy hand. In the corner of the one window, a spider has worked a web – a scalloped interlacing of delicate pattern. Sadly, twisting inconsequentially, a large, fluffy moth is doomed to its fate. I look away, uncomfortable, and listen to the final movement of the Bruch.

Still stupid thoughts niggle. I am not ready for the wheelchair and the boiled fish. The invincible grey is hennaed, the whiskers are whisked and the armies of facial lines ignored, together with the flushes and the dozy brain days. I am fifty-three but I still feel a voluptuous woman, even sexy. I need sexual love. Joseph and I need to make love; that part of our lives is good; the children would be shocked. With the new mantle of 'grandmother' does that all go, submerged in a welter of baby wipes and warm bottles?

Will I cope? Will it love me? Will I be a satisfactory grandma?

And the important fears stay, the new responsibilities, the new anxieties. I was always one of those that worried about the planet. Recycling mad, using the right products. But now caring for the earth means much more. I want this little one to see all the animals, not just the few that are preserved in zoo museums. It should one day be able to walk in a meadow as my parents did and their parents before them, enjoying wild flowers, red poppies, golden buttercups under a chubby chin, delicate scabious, vivid cornflowers. I want that child, as its right, to be able to walk in safety: see and touch a landscape. Hear a skylark's bubbling ascension, pick blackberries and eat them with blue-stained fingers: jump and swim in the sea and laugh at the briny waves, and go rock pooling, trousers rolled as I did and my children did.

And as a future grandmother, hoping, praying all goes well, grandmother to a mere heartbeat right now, I have my camera ready and I will bore my friends with endless packs of thirty-six. I will do gluing and painting and babysitting and all the grandma specialities. I will be superb. I will fight for this little one because I am a creator of tradition. I know the past and I will give it to the future.

CLOWNING AROUND

It's her birthday. She's five today. She's lucky. She's had her very own parcel in the post from her Gran with books and games and a Barbie doll. Aunty Catrin sent a real fairy outfit from the Disney shop, and her Mummy and Daddy bought a new coat and special clothes for her party and a big girl's bike with stabilisers on it. The bike had strings of glitter on the front handle... handlebars that twinkled like Christmas when she pushed it down the hallway. It was a lovely party. Her Daddy tied pink balloons to the tops of the furniture with silver ribbons and she wore her new jeans with purple sparkle on the bottom. She played Pass the Parcel, Musical Chairs and danced to her new CD before tea. Then they had burgers and chips, red pop, crisps and choc-ices. There was a cake made like a rabbit sleeping in a bed with his feet sticking out at the end. She didn't want her Mummy to cut the cake, because it would spoil him so they lifted up his icing covers and saved just the icing rabbit. He's safe on a saucer in the pantry. Then they all had some of the cake and everybody sang *Happy Birthday*.

After tea, Daddy dressed up as a clown in an outfit from a shop and painted his face white with a red shiny nose and smiling mouth. Jessica had a real clown at her party but Mummy said they were too expensive. Daddy was very funny. He did some magic. He took fifty pence out of her ear and pulled hankies from a hat and made Jessica, Amber and Jasmine laugh. Then Jonathan started to show off and ran around and around the room and got dizzy and was sick over the couch and it was time for her friends to go home. She wanted to have a proper ride with her new bike, so Daddy took her out after the party for a few minutes in the park. She asked Mummy to take her, but Mummy said she was too busy. Daddy's lost his job – she has to work on the computer in the evenings. They tried out the bike and Daddy held her very tight round her tummy. But she doesn't need him to hold her. She kept telling him, 'Let me go. I can do it myself. It's easy'. But he still held her. Then she was tired and they went home and she was allowed to eat her supper in her pyjamas in front of the telly as a treat.

She is five years and one week old. Daddy says he's putting her to bed while Mummy's at her 'robics class. First he bathed her in the bath with Jonathan. He scrubbed really hard – it hurt a bit. He said she was dirty from playing. But she didn't go in the garden because it was wet. She'd only played with Plasticine and her new dolls, and her best pop-up book with the pictures of the clowns with red noses. When Mummy bathes her she bathes her on her own. She calls it 'girls time', and makes her hair into punky spikes and pointy witch's horns with foam and sometimes they have a whole bottle of bubbles and blow big bendy balls that bang on her and burst.

Daddy lets her stay up – really late; he says it's a special treat because she is such a good girl and they have fish fingers and Jammy Dodgers. They watch *Coronation Street* and *Family Fortunes*. He's making jokes and playing with her new Barbie – lifting up her dress. She wants Mummy to come home. Daddy has a funny face like when a bit of bread sticks in your throat. She wants Mummy home. 'When will Mummy be back? Will she be long? I WANT HER TO COME HOME.' But Daddy laughs, says she shouldn't be a baby now she is five, and plays the new game of squashing her on the couch. She doesn't like it.

It's her seventh birthday today and the summer holidays. When Mummy opened her bedroom curtains this morning, the sunlight washed over her bed and covered her dolls with glimmer dust and chased away the dark. She can wear her new lilac shorts and T-shirt. They are going to have a birthday picnic at Roath Park. Mummy is taking the whole day off. She didn't ask her friends because she never gets Mummy for a whole day. First she and Mummy buy fried chicken and extra rolls and Tango. Then they take some blankets and some chairs from the garden and lay them out beside the water. She has a clown cake with large red lips. It is smiling. But she doesn't like it. She doesn't say but she doesn't mind when it is cut up and the face is spoilt.

After tea Daddy takes Jonathan to try out his fishing rod. It's a long pole with a little basket on the end. Jonathan is so excited. Mummy has a large plastic container ready for all the fish, but they only catch a few beetles and a water snail and some slimy weed. She sits with Mummy. She lets her hang her legs over the bank so she can swing them. She wants to say...

Then Mummy sees a kingfisher.

'Look, darling. Stay very very still and you'll see it. It's on that branch close to the water just past the dark shadow. See its orange belly and throat and turquoise-blue wings.'

'Yes yes. It's so tiny – lovely colours.'

It sits for a while as they watch it, pushing in its feathers with a long pointy beak, and they are so quiet she can feel the banging in her chest. Then it shrieks loudly and flies off like a blue firework and is gone.

'That was so beautiful,' says Mummy. 'It's lucky to see a kingfisher – they are so rare down here now. Our luck must be turning. Maybe Daddy will start looking for another job again, eh?'

But Daddy comes back and hears what Mummy has said, and they start arguing again. She wants them to stop. Then Jonathan starts to cry and the day goes grey. They carry home the stuff and when they get in, Mummy makes them some beans on toast and goes to bed. She says she has a headache. They were going to play Monopoly. She'd promised. But perhaps she is too upset. Daddy gets out the whisky from the cupboard and pours out a big glass and puts on a CD really loud. After she's had her bath, she knocks on Mummy's door to see if her pain has gone. She thought she heard crying. But she doesn't like to go in. Jonathan puts his hands over his ears and starts to cry too, so she goes in his room and they read from his new book. He stops crying. She gets into the little bed next to him that they have for his friends to stay and then he is better. She hears Daddy's feet on the landing and knows he's come into the room, so she pretends she is asleep. She can smell the whisky and his smoke... but then he turns and walks out and switches off the light.

Last week she had her ninth birthday. Daddy took Amber, Jonathan and her to the circus. They queued for ages and when they walked in to the Big Top it smelt of damp and crushed grass. She was happy because she sat next to Amber and Daddy sat next to Jonathan. She loved the white horses – their manes plaited with shimmery ribbons and their tails swishing as they galloped to the music. She was glad there weren't any tigers and lions and she wished they didn't make the elephant do tricks. But the trapeze artists were brilliant, swaying so high up and catching each other to the music. Their faces were made up with swirls of green and black and they wore pearly leotards that changed colour with the lights. Then the drums rolled and, at the very top of the tent, a tiny lady dressed in red glitter chiffon climbed onto the shoulders of a man who sat on a bike holding a long post across the handle bars, and rode slowly across the empty space. They were all so worried and the music was scary. She was glad when they reached the other side. In between each act, the clowns came out, playing with cars and throwing water over each other. Everyone else laughed. But she still doesn't like clowns. On the way home they had pizzas and took one back for Mummy. But she wasn't home when they got back and Daddy got cross – again.

She went to bed with one of her new books and then she heard footsteps outside her room... A band of light edged her door and she wanted to call out to Mummy, but she knew she was still at her conference. She wished Mummy were home.

She's thirteen. They had a special assembly today. After prayers, a lady and a gentleman arrived to talk to them. She was really pleased because they said that the talk would last for half the morning and she would miss double maths. The girls and the boys were separated and they stayed in the hall and the boys were led into the gym. They had to move forward towards the stage and the lady sat on the edge of the stage. Then the film projector was pulled out and she was thrilled. They were going to watch a film in the morning! Amber is still in her class and they sat next to each other. She hugged her.

'This is better than double maths,' she whispered.

'Yes, anything's better than double maths.'

They both giggled until Mrs Kennedy frowned at them. The lady began to talk in a soft voice about what people can do to you, where they might touch you and how you must say 'no'. Then they pulled the curtains in the hall so it was quite dark. The video started. Hollow echoing voices. She knew the story. A squeezing began inside her chest and a lump grew in her throat. She didn't want to cry in front of the others. She had to stop them.

'Please, Miss. Can I be excused?'

She flew down the corridor to the toilets – a smell of wee. Opened a cubicle door, pushed inside banging one leg against the cold pedestal, locked it and let the tears out. She blubbered like Jonathan when he fell off his big bike. Her blouse was soaked and her nose and eyes were streaming. Then she heard Amber calling.

'Are you all right?'

'Yes, I'm fine.'

'Yeeh, you sound it! Come on out... we'll talk.'

They walked to the playground. Amber put her arm around her shoulders. The wall was cold and slimy from the rain. But they sat on it together. She told Amber about the night visits, only bits though. It's too hard to say it all. She didn't mean to do any harm. Amber's her best friend.

'Honestly, Mummy. I swear. Amber promised she wouldn't tell. I only told her because I was so desperate to talk to someone. I didn't think that she would speak to her mum and this would happen. I'm not bad. I didn't tell. I swear I didn't tell the lady or the man, or the people that came to our house.'

BAGGAGE

'We were lucky they didn't weigh our stuff,' says Joseph, falling back on the metal seat belt clasps, grimacing and mopping a tanned forehead. 'We've brought back half of Italy.' He carefully hands a new watercolour painting, bubble wrapped, to the hostess to stow at the back of the aircraft and squeezes the travel documents into a leather holdall jammed full of duty free.

We laugh with relief as he pulls the seat belt away from his sore rump and we attempt to get comfortable in our cramped space.

'Maybe it'll stay empty,' he says, eyeing the aisle seat next to him.

Then a woman takes it and her partner sits on the other side of the gangway, followed by a group of elderly people joking and laughing. The woman clicks the seat belt into place and from over her shoulders she carefully manoeuvres a Shaun-the-Sheep haversack.

She sits it in her lap facing her, its large plastic eyes gazing blankly, and gently adjusts the black velveteen legs into a crossed position, resting the body carefully against the seat back.

We smile, a polite acknowledgement, and I notice a late forties face where a bright summer is fading fast, fair but golden skin sprinkled with freckles and water green eyes.

The tannoy begins the safety spiel, with the air hostesses doing their puppet-like imitations, opening and closing the seat belt, putting on a life jacket, and pretending to blow it up. I sit rigid and clasp Joseph's hand tightly. My fingers tense with the noting of emergency exits, slides and crash positions. We are told to examine the shiny cardboard safety regulations. I cross them in a small prayer. If I read everything, pay attention and try to be as virtuous as I can for the next year, I promise, I promise...

'Come on, girl,' Joseph says. 'They do it every day and they're not scared. You can handle it. If we don't do this bit, we don't get to Italy.'

I try to listen to the logical part of my mind. Flying is the safest way of travelling – they keep saying so. I'm a reasonably intelligent woman – why?

'Bad news, folks,' calls the pilot. 'According to air traffic control, we are going to have to wait an extra half hour for our slot.'

More nerves. The plane is sticky hot, the air conditioning ineffectual against a thirty-seven degrees Verona tarmac.

But, eventually, we take off. Within seconds, Verona is a Lego-land of toy houses and cars which mutate into an animated map. My ears pop and I try not to think of those emergency exits or the weight of the plane that stays in the air with nothing beneath it except soft grey and white clouds that look like the ragged wool catchings that hang on the valley bushes at home.

'There you are, Shaun. You'll be alright now,' says the woman beside my husband.

He's relaxed with a fortnight's sun, good living and Italian music and picks up her conversation. 'Doesn't he like flying?' he humours.

'Oh no,' she says seriously. 'He's very nervous, but he's had a lovely holiday. We even managed to get him his hat.'

Jaunty, cartoon-faced, Shaun watches his guardian. Perched on the top of his woolly head is a hat, a tiny child-size imitation boater, perfectly fashioned in traditional straw with "Venetia" written in gaudy red ribbon in the fashion of the gondoliers.

'He wanted one last year when we were in Venice but we didn't have the time – there were so many galleries and buildings to see and of course when you are on an organised coach trip with other people it's so difficult to break away and do your own thing.'

We nod, a little apprehensive. Joseph nudges the side of my leg with a discreet little finger.

'He sulked for a whole year and we promised him that we would try again. Anyway, this time we were able to manage a little freedom. We took advantage of a spare day and went to Venice.'

'Did you manage to see the Doge's Palace?' I ask, thinking of our pilgrimages to the Hall of the Pregadi, the Senate hall with lavish gilded walls adorned with the works of Jacopo and Domenico Tintoretto and Jacopo Palma the Younger. The memories of aching necks accompanied by gasps as we marvelled at the

Veroneses swirling with partly clothed cupids, landscapes and elaborately dressed figures, magnificently executed. And then the Bellini Christ Mourned, so ahead of its time, in the Ducal apartment.

'We really wanted to but we had promised Shaun and the purpose of the day was to get his hat. I'm not saying we didn't get a lovely lunch out of it. But a promise is a promise isn't it, Shaun?' With a cuddle and a squeeze, she turns the haversack so its back rests against her body, bending and placing the legs until she is satisfied.

A drinks trolley moves up the aisle to us. 'Would you like a juice, apple or orange, before your meal?' An attractive black airhostess with fair highlights leans over.

'Apple, please,' says our companion.

As the hostess passes the plastic glass, she looks down over at the haversack. 'That's Shaun the sheep,' she exclaims in a thick East End accent. 'They're wonderful aren't they? I've got one of those on the back of my car. You know, he nods his head? I like the trainers – they're so cute.' She moves on to apple-and-orange juice the rest of the passengers.

'Oh but he's not the same, he's... ' Discomfort twists the slim body. She crosses and uncrosses her legs, repeatedly grazing slim fingers over the light beige cotton fabric of her dress. The pale green eyes darken and she looks as if she is pinned and bleeding, an impaled butterfly.

I feel compassion and edge towards her anxieties, my own forgotten. 'I love the shoes,' I say, trying to encourage her. 'Did you buy them specially?' I look at the minute baby shoes – first size, white with miniature ABCs written around their edges and small perfectly tied laces.

'Oh yes,' she answers gratefully, 'and he has a sheepskin jacket for the winter. He likes it because then I don't have to wash him so much. He hates being washed, complains like mad, because he smells all girly when he comes out of the machine and he absolutely loathes that!'

By this time the hostesses are bringing small trays of food. We are lucky. My husband looks at tomato and mozzarella salad decorated with fresh basil sprigs, a small crispy side salad, crunchy roll full of toasted seeds and a fresh fruit salad – the vegetarian option – and I am given a pasta salad with asparagus and mushrooms, the vegan meal. 'Lovely lunch for airport food,' he mumbles as he dips his fork appreciatively. He glances at his neighbour. 'Aren't you having? It's really good. You can tell they've made it in Italy – not the usual rubber rolls and lukewarm creations we get on the outward journey.'

'No,' says the woman. 'We can't. It wouldn't be fair to Shaun. He would be so uncomfortable if we put the flap down. He hates lying down and it might even squash him. It's better just to do without.'

Across the aisle, her partner has also refused his meal. 'Just coffee,' he says to the airhostess, an anxious hand pushed through the depths of thick hair and a young face furrowed with anxieties. 'We won't be long now, Shaun,' he says reaching for one of the small legs and giving it an affectionate tweak.

'Drink, Sir, with your meal?'

'Red, please,' says Joseph, perhaps recalling glorious bottles of Bardolino supped in sleepy piazzas. He pours out the wine, tastes it and looks at our companion. 'The wine's quite good,' he says. 'It's not rough.'

'No, we won't drink in front of Shaun because then he'll want a drink and he gets silly if he drinks and we'll have a terrible job with him after that. And he's quite spoilt, he'll only drink Irish whiskey, so we only let him drink occasionally at home when he's just with us.'

By now my husband is embarrassed. He says stiffly. 'Have you got far to go, then?'

'Yes, when we get back to Gatwick we have to make our way back to France, practically the same route back. It's a nuisance but when you go on an organised coach trip, they can't make any arrangements for individuals.'

'Do you live in France?'

'Yes, we've lived there for fifteen years. We love it. We live in one of the wine regions, beautiful country – very quiet, what we want, really.' She pushes some straggles of hair that have escaped the scrunchy with a slim, pale hand traced with a network of fine blue veins.

As she speaks, I touch her tragedy, her secret. I'm aware of a white deadness, a shroud-wrapped past, the absence of a child. The still vacuum fights with my own post-holiday euphoria. I return to two grown-up children, our daughter now married and expecting her first child. We are to be grandparents for the first time. Our cases are loaded with presents. A new dress for my daughter with room to expand, a pair of shoes for her, two handbags, a briefcase for my son, T-shirts for my son-in-law and son and a good belt, and aftershave and sweets and aprons with pasta painted on their kitschy fronts and scarves and...

The plane begins to shake – we are experiencing turbulence. We are told to return to our seats and fasten our seat belts. The crew don't seem anxious. I watch them pushing trolleys of duty free, and screw in my fancy earplugs to stop the pain. In an effort to contain the growing terror, the tight, choking fear within my chest, I stare out of the window and try to concentrate on the changing view. Now the clouds are transformed to grey, lumpy palaces, cities that fight and buffet our small jet.

I glance back at our companion. She doesn't seem troubled by the shake of the plane, the slight cracking noises. She sits serene reading her novel, clutching the object of her love. Was it only last year that Concorde crashed with one hundred and thirteen dead? I must be sensible. We are pushing through walls and floors of leaden, impenetrable, altocumulus then cumulus. Will we ever land? Finally, down, down, down to a faint green. Through the grizzled taupe new micro lands appear, festooned with mini houses and trees. Joseph's hand clutches mine in sympathy. He knows how I feel. As we twist and bend in the last turns, I rest my clammy head on the side of the plane. At last there is a bumping and a pulling back, a burst of noise and energy. I see the flaps on the wings of the aircraft open to brake. We have made it. The woman refolds her book with a slight sigh and looks at her partner, then at the pretend animal. 'There you are, Shaun,' she says. 'It wasn't really so bad, was it?' She smiles at us with pity in her face.

'You poor thing,' she says. 'You really suffer, don't you?'

'Yes, I hate it.'

She gathers her possessions together watching me, tasting my terror, embracing Shaun.

'Safe journey,' says Joseph.

'Thank you for travelling with British Airways. We hope you've enjoyed your flight,' says the tannoy in a thick East End accent.

RED STILETTOS

How it all began. I'm standing in my chef's whites, just one woman: the new sous-chef battling in a stainless-steel dungeon they call a kitchen. Chef tastes my nervousness. Then sniffs the scent like a dog and plans his strategy. Over time, I've gained the others' respect. 'She's not bad – a good mate,' they say to each other as they loll on the concrete steps behind the restaurant, after service, enjoying the intake of a quick roll-up.

But he is different. He takes advantage – bullying me, knowing that his superior position gives him extra power. When the others are outside, he gives me extra work, at the sinks. Out of sight. Then, when I am sharpening the knives, he steals behind me, trying to slip his greasy fingers between my loose chef's garments to feel my skin. Once, just once, when the cleaver was in my hand, and he had moved against me again with his turgid swollen body stinking of garlic and smoke, the temptation to slash and cut was so

93

strong, I realised I was changing as a person – that he was turning me into his monster. I hated him so much and thought about leaving almost every second. But it is a good job – well paid – and the references when I leave could give me the chance to move on, to Paris, New York, Sydney perhaps. Certainly to a top position in one of the best restaurants in London. So I know I just have to manage, to think about the future and leave, one day, with the best references. In the meantime, I have to endure the constant cruelties.

It was inevitable. Finally he broke all the rules.

He had been strangely quiet that day, no jokes about choppers and other filth and I was grateful. After the lunch-time service, stupidly, I began to hope that after so much rejection, he had decided to abandon his games. I was caught unawares. For just that day I forgot to double fasten my possessions in my locker and popped my handbag under the counter. It must have been a simple matter to take my key from the bunch and get it copied – that's my only explanation...

We were late that night. A party arrived after the theatre. Upstairs was filled with boozy laughter. I love to see the dressed-up clothes and knew after the number of cases of Krug, and Moet, followed by all those bottles of Chateauneuf-du-Pape, no one would notice me standing in the wings. So I sneaked upstairs. Against the rules but hey, they all did it. There were groups of them, laughing and talking loudly. Men in evening dress, women, mainly in black, fired with diamonds. One woman wore a grey silk chiffon dress, the softness and colour of pigeon feathers. Its fine pleats curled around her body licking her curves and with it she wore a pair of red stilettos.

They were six inches, at least, pushing her hips forward and so high that that they forced her to rest from time to time, at the side of a table. I knew those shoes – those red stilettos. I had studied their form on many occasions as an artist revels in a painting or sculpture. Those exquisite shoes were not just shoes but this season's Manolo Blahniks – the ultimate red stiletto – the sweep of the heel height so carefully balanced to offset the rounded peep-toe, the whole draped with the finest suede kid. My ultimate dream shoe. I read all the glossies. At the end of a long evening's prepping and service, there was nothing quite like a warm bath, a glass of wine and really good mag. When others fantasised over pop stars, film stars, nights of champagne in Paris or sipping Bellini's in Harry's Bar in Venice, I dreamt of shoes – stilettos in particular. Even after work when my legs were heavy with the pain of standing, I still wore my black stilettos to go home. I love the tap-tap staccato of heels on concrete – that feeling of being utterly a woman.

That night, I walked back to my flat contemplating the prospect of a warm bath, a good glass of red, and the velvety tones of Barry White. I've always loved my flat. It's what they call a studio flat and has a bonus of a secure courtyard, a hunting-ground for my cat and a popular place for a barbecue, a plus in a large city. I pushed open the door. Damn, I should have recognised his foulness, a repugnant mix of sweat, smoke and grease. My only excuse was that I was tired and it all happened so quickly. He was waiting for me in the darkness. I heard a rustle behind me. I wanted to scream but the terror choked my throat. Before I was fully aware, one stinking arm was about my neck and he was trying to pull my body into

95

a lock. But I managed to turn. I was inches away from his face. I noticed a froth of spit on the corners of his thick, purplish lips. Call me crazy but it was the spit that galvanised me. With a rapid movement I snapped up a knee and aimed a blow below his ugly belly. I think his clothes must have been undone. After this, there was a strange animal grunting sound as he released his lock on my neck, bending forward, followed by gasping and moaning. His face was on its side. I pulled off one of my stilettos and stabbed the heel in the grizzled squashed bristles of his cheek. A boiling ugly hatred deepened my voice to a growl.

'You want me. Do you?'

Suddenly he looked vulnerable. I continued to grind the stiletto into him. He lay on the floor at my feet. Crumpled, pathetic.

'Yes... yes, I want you.'

'Well, this is no way to get me.'

My mind was racing. It must have been adrenaline, plus the hours I had spent at the sink and steel tables yearning for revenge. Or the perfect joy of kneeing and felling the monster that suddenly focussed my mind into thoughts.

'You can have me,' I said. 'But I want the perfect reference. Because after you possess me, I will never return to work with you again. Is that clear?'

Underneath my hands he was a grovelling jelly of ugliness. He whimpered agreement. I think it had to be the shock of the moment – the sudden turn of events inspired by my cheap black stilettos now ruined, that motivated my last demand.

'My final request is a pair of red stilettos – you will buy them for me. This season's Manolo Blahniks in red suede. Nothing else will do. You will have the reference and the shoes ready in a size thirty-nine, and then I will give you what you want.'

He breathed agreement.

'In the meantime, you will not touch me or I will report you to the police. Your fingerprints must be all over this flat. And your blood on my shoe which will go in my boyfriend's safe when you leave... which is now.'

He crept onto his knees and I watched his disgusting body crawl to the front door, over the beautiful Victorian tiles I had taken so long to restore. Hobbling to the entrance, with one final burst of strength, I kicked him out of my flat with my other shoe, and slammed the door. I felt clammy, cold. Sick with shock. I switched on all the lights. I began to shudder and shake. Gulping sobs that would not stop. I ran to the bathroom tearing off clothes that would have to be burnt, jamming them with my stiletto into a black plastic bag. Then I was in the bath with the water too hot, scrubbing. Trying to obliterate, annihilate, eradicate his smell, the touch of his doughy skin, the invasion of my space, my home, my life. Scrubbing with soap and a nailbrush until my skin was red-raw. How would I cope? Would I ever be able to return to work? I needed that reference to move on. I had to remain strong.

That night, I had the locks changed and drank the rest of a bottle of brandy saved for a good celebration. How I managed to get to work the next day still remains a miracle. But I knew the boys would be sympathetic if I told them Chef had tried something on. I didn't specify. He didn't come in, that day or for the rest of the week. We ran the kitchen without him.

On Thursday we were told that Elliot Barnard, the new food critic for one of the Sundays, would pay us a visit and, unlike some of his colleagues, he liked to give us fair warning. Maybe it was because he enjoyed perfection or perhaps it was because the company advertised heavily in that paper and he wanted to give us a good write-up. Whatever the reason, we were prepared. I was asked by the proprietor, Mr Edmonton, to run the service. It was my chance and I was glad of the challenge – something to occupy my mind. With the proprietor's permission, I made some changes of my own. I had done my homework. This critic was originally from Australia and was passionate about fusion food. He loved to see conventions broken. Classical was reliable, but could be staid. I planned to bring the 1970s menu into the twenty-first century.

I began with the fish soup, which was a standard bouillabaisse. It was good. It was prepared with a good mixture of fresh fish, tomatoes and saffron, but recently it had lacked popularity and had sat on the menu, un-chosen, superfluous like a wallflower at a party. I decided to infuse the fish with a marinade of freshly ground Thai spices, chopped ginger, curry leaves, galangal, coriander leaves, and chopped red shiny bird's eye chillies. Then remove the fire with rich, fresh coconut milk. As I dished the golden soup into the bowl, for seconds I stopped, wondering about his reaction, and for that matter, what Mr Edmonton would think of his new menu. I took a deep breath and added the decoration of spring onion and chilli flowers – red chillies split down their sides and whole large tiger prawns. Then sent it with Michel, our top and most experienced waiter. I need not have worried.

Previously it had always been solid British fare for the main course. Which was good in its own right, though the slices of rare roast beef bleeding on the plate were even too rare for me. But Elliot Barnard had a passion for light food with a concentration of flavour. So I took some lamb chops, letting them sit in a good red wine with thyme, rosemary, balsamic vinegar and olive oil before grilling them quickly on the griddle. Then I sliced them finely and laid them on a bed of roquette and crisp fennel slices. Barnard also ordered the chicken breast, which can be dry, but I stuffed the beaten out breasts, rolled them with a wild mushroom filling and poached them gently, presenting them for service surrounded by steamed baby vegetables.

For seconds the clattering bang of the kitchen became silent as we waited for the reaction. Michel returned with his thumbs up and a smile that said our team had won.

Then onto the finale and my special new Cappuccino Panacotta – a wobbling smooth cooked confection made with fromage frais rather than cream, an iced lemon tart on the thinnest of pastry, sharp with the tang of specially purchased Sicilian lemons, and a strawberry and black pepper granita — well laced with framboise liqueur. Michel came down from the dining room again, laughing, and the boys roared with satisfaction. I knew Barnard was happy.

After the service, I changed into fresh whites to meet Mr Barnard. For a man who wielded such immense power, he was small of stature with dark hair slightly thinning on the top, but his eyes were a vivid blue, the colour of his beloved Barrier Reef.

'This is a change from the last time I visited,' he enthused as he shook my hand with a powerful grasp.

'Modern, original and downright tasty, yes tasty.' He turned to Mr Edmonton. 'Got rid of the old bloke, did you? Good food but a bit boring, predictable – this girl's got imagination, flair.' Mr Edmonton was nodding and smiling.

Honestly, all I'd wanted from that effort was a good reference. I'd been happy to challenge my brain and draw on my enthusiasm. All those years at the sink I'd thought of the changes we could make but Chef was so self-opinionated and bombastic.

The following week Chef returned. The boys told me he'd been on another blinder. I had dreaded his appearance, a confrontation. But I had warned the boys and they were ready. He sidled into the kitchen dressed in a filthy T-shirt and worn leather jacket and handed me a large bag containing a box – a shoe box in a special dust-cover – and an envelope which I scanned quickly. Yes, my reference written in a scrawl on grubby paper.

Of course he would get nothing in return. He must have known that as he crawled away from my flat. The box and the reference were my payment for silence.

That night I walked back to my flat and after the perfect bath laced with rose and patchouli oils, I dried myself. Shivering with excitement I removed the box slowly from its luxurious dustcover, running my fingers slowly over the black classical writing *Manolo Blahnik*, the most silken tissue, and finally the shoes, revelling in their glorious beauty, their height, their luscious curves, from heel to toe. I slowly slipped on the shoes and felt the angle of my body changed, cantilevered into new heights of elegance. I looked at myself as I stood naked in front of the mirror wearing just the dream shoes – my red stilettos.

EATING FOR TWO

Imagine a bowl of summer fruit, an abundance of peaches, nectarines and apricots plucked from dappled orchards, and, nestling among them, a few lychees. Travellers from the Orient. Foreigners. You know their taste and they tempt. But fresh, they are difficult to manage. A hard crisp outer case that peels like an eggshell and, discarded, looks like lizard skin. Then the sharp-sweet taste and, further within, a smooth brown nut, inedible. Shiny. Important. Looks to a gardener as if it would grow immediately into a vast tree with polished shiny leaves, or form the counter in an exotic game. You succumb. Your fingers crack the shell open with a snap. The juice runs. You have bruised it. You bite into the chewy flesh, run your tongue around the polished seed, and then discard it, rattling on a plate.

But there is a time when you need to go beyond. To hold that seed. Understand its value.

It's the holiday season at last. The long dark ache of November to February has given way to the summer light of August. Our annual pilgrimage to the Italian lakes arrives. For two weeks I can pretend that I am a local. Sip rich black Americanos in lakeside cafes. Practice my halting Italian with indulgent friends. Drink too much red and white wine, their claret and honey colours bright as the conversation.

This year, though, I carry with me a weight, an unearthed guilt. At home we are downsizing, and the package I inherited on my mother's untimely death, in 1971, that my husband tactfully moved into the loft, will re-emerge and must be dealt with, along with all the detritus of living for twenty four years in the same home.

Friends who have already condensed their lives into the confines of a flat fail to understand my predicament. Their reasoning is that of people who can easily discard valentines, children's first drawings, the plastic frogs little ones bought with spending money when they went on a school trip which say *to the best Mum in the world.* 'You've just got to be ruthless,' they pronounce, with reasoned intellect.

Over a dinner of fresh tomato soup heavily scented with basil, gnocchi with a wild mushroom sauce, fresh salad and peaches to follow, my husband and I talk. He has lived with my inherited agony and feels my ordeal.

'Don't think about it,' he says. 'You're on holiday. When you're back is time enough. I'll help you. We'll sort it together.'

I wish I could just pretend the thing was not there. But it is, and it is mine alone to conquer. At every waking moment she lives with me. I still hear her cries. In my mind, the empty bed still holds the voice. Her treasured art books sit in my study – the pages hold images of her shaking bone-thin fingers. Her favourite music still brings easy tears – she always wanted Elgar's Enigma Variations, the Nimrod section, or Grieg's Piano Concerto, the same choices as Princess Diana. Bizarre – two women with tragedy sealed into their lives. I can be out, with family, enjoying, and I will see a silhouette, a twist of a blonde head, smell a familiar fragrance – a French perfume she loved to wear, even in bed wrapped in bed-jackets to fight her constant chill – see a malnourished body and in seconds I am trying to revive a skeleton. When I eat, I know her terror and taste her refusal. And when my children were sick I used to make the same liquidised arrowroot-peach gruel that sometimes rescued her from another bout in hospital. But it cannot go on. It is time to get to the nub, the seed, the stone, and deal with it.

When we return he will bring out the parcel from the loft. It contains a small broken suitcase secured with twine. Inside, a diary written by a little girl of twelve arriving in a strange country, accompanied only by an older brother, both terrified. Without a familiar tongue, with a family abandoned in a distant country, and the terror of imminent death in their consciousness.

The diary is covered in a rough orange and brown tweed fabric and has a small brass lock but no key. I can see her writing. Small careful strokes in her adopted language. It reads:

I arrived at a station. There were a lot of people standing around. I knew none of them. They moved me with my brother off

105

the train and he was called by a lady with a list and placed with some people – a religious family. He was terrified. We needed to be together. He turned around just once. I saw his face. It spoke my fear, and then he dropped his head and left with his new people. I was left alone. Would someone love me? A lady came up to me. She was wearing a lot of makeup and a strange hat with a feather that sat over one eye. She kissed me and said that she would be my Aunt. I think I was expected to kiss her but she was a stranger.

I remember the first time I sat next to her empty chair, a large broad-backed dralon laden with pillows to soften the pains from pressure sores, the day after her burial, in the time of Jewish mourning. My father, choking with the bitterness of it, hurled her box of jewellery at my feet, along with this small suitcase. With swollen eyes, I shook as I found a book filled with bureaucrat's stamps and archaic German writing – her official papers – and a parcel label that went around her childish neck. Human luggage.

She never recovered. At fifteen she was declared an enemy alien and had to report to the police station weekly. She could not bear the humiliation. The authorities insisted that she should leave her foster mother and take employment. She worked as a skivvy, in service, just to obtain kosher food. But she could not cope with the brutality 'below stairs', and falsified her age to join the fire-service. Even then her life remained unhappy. She met my father and they clung together, their only links in the fragile raft of marriage ownership of the same religion, and knowledge of a more familiar and comfortable tongue.

Her unhappiness was tangible. At first she tried to make a success of her life but an operation for breast cancer when I was five meant that she had to retire from the small fashion business she had developed and leave it in my father's care. He began to take the collection around the country, I suspect, to disappear from a fraught marriage. She was weak and felt that her femininity had been cut out of her, leaving no purpose to her life. She began to stop eating and I became her nurse, and stomach. Was it solely a cry for help or, maybe, a growing sense of culpability – a discomfort with her easy access to food?

I have no memory of a mother who went with me to shop for a dress, or sat at a table and ate a normal meal. Ours was a sequence of dance movements and the steps were set. My father, a frustrated pressure cooker ready to explode, would curse. My mother would begin crying, followed by choking, then blaming, and begin to throw up her food. My father would panic and scream at me, often storming out of the house, and I would have to nurse the sobbing, vomiting, vestige of a body, trying to restore some calm. I'd hold that husk of skin-wrapped bird-bones, and promise not to leave, ever. And sometimes, although I loved her, I hated her too, because she was my jailer. The music of that dance became more frequent and insistent the older we both became. But the orchestration that produced the most exquisite fugues were newsreels from Germany, a German marching song, the sight of a German flag.

I was too young to remember the day she discovered her father and mother had been murdered in an ice forest in Riga, where they dug their own graves and those of their three children who ran with them. But I lived her pain every day.

Compliant, and trapped, I would cook and eat for her. To salve her sorrows and her need to feed and be fed, I ate for two. Her health deteriorated. As I swelled to fourteen and a half stone, she shrank to four. Eventually, her only pleasure was for me to carry her into the kitchen where she would direct from a chair and watch me cook and eat.

But my guilt became more finite. Something clicked – call it hormones, the snap of the elastic band of 'yes'. I was seventeen and hated my shape. I refused to eat for peace any more. I could no longer live in that prison of a body. Soon, slimmer and more attractive, I met my future husband. We wanted to marry and, three years later, after numerous arguments, hysterical sick bouts, and emergency trips to hospital, I left. I had to choose. Was I wrong? I tried to keep everyone happy. Every day I walked the mile to her house. I became pregnant and when I had my baby, I pushed the pram round and nursed her, carrying her to the toilet, many times a day. Until, eighteen months later, she died. I was with my husband getting an emergency prescription when it happened, unaware that he was trying to spare me her final moments.

My father dragged me by the hair up the stairs. Pushed my terrified body on to her twisted face and screamed 'murderer!' I lost our second baby a week later, but Dad remained unforgiving. That was 1971.

*　　　　　*　　　　　*

We are lucky. We have wonderful Italian friends who are taking us to the Parco Giardino Sigurta, just outside Mantova. It is a magnificent park resonant with the sound of birdsong and brave in its use of colour. Only the Italians have the courage to place clashing purple bougainvillea with red acers and orange and gold cannas. Water-gardens flow and bubble as orange koi carp slip through their depths, and scarlet water hibiscus dip their toes on the edges of pools of limpid water. We are stunned by the sight of violet, yellow and cerise water lilies floating proudly – confident of their elegance. Then, as we near the *finale* of the seven-kilometre walk, hot and breathless, we see lotus flowers growing in a shaded pool. Delicate pink flowers rising tall as a man, out of silent water, their heads the size of an adult's head with circular leaves like platters. The Far East sleeping in the Mediterranean sun. It is possible to adapt.

I have tried before to understand the problem and cope with it. On the sixtieth anniversary of the Kinder-transport, I went to London to see if there were people who remembered my mother when she was a child. To discover another facet to her personality. I knew she was a talented artist, could sing, sew, crochet and cook. There were tantalising moments when... it was essential to find the missing pieces of the jigsaw. The first lectures were interesting. Successful survivors talking about their experiences when they arrived in their adopted country. Then it was lunchtime. We all made our way into a vast dining room where tables were laid out and labelled according to the town of origin of the person. I had my mother's maiden name written on a sticker on my chest. A woman in her seventies sat next to me. She stared at me. Muttered the name written on the label. I felt confident that she would know my mother and that she could replace the images I had with a kinder vision.

'Did you know her?' I asked. 'Did you know my mother and her family?'

'Of course I knew the family. He was the Chief Rabbi... wonderful, cultured people – their house was always filled with the most interesting individuals. Artists, musicians, philosophers.'

This was no surprise. I'd read the books, recognised the approbation. Then, as the meal progressed, survivors on zimmers and in wheel chairs began to call out, over a microphone, names of those missing. Still trying to unearth some evidence of life after so many years. My dinner companion continued staring at me until, suddenly, she leaned over into my space and cupped my face in her hands.

'You are not her. You are Ruth. One of the dead ones murdered in Riga!'

I am named after my dead Aunt Ruth. I reeled back in shock as she continued.

'You are her and she is dead.'

I fled from the room, and my ghosts with sepia faces. Escaped from that place of survivors, to the safety of my husband's side. Hours later, I could still heard her words, see her haunted eyes in my mind.

*   *   *

It's Ferragusto. The main Italian feast day. We have decided to walk to Bardolino through the campsites, to our destination in the main street, to the best and crispiest pizza, a fresh salad and a half bottle of good local wine. The dusty path is full of people in bathing costumes and towels making their way to their piece of rock or patch of grass. The sun is hot on our backs.

We pass the German campsites and the air is rich with the scent of coconut suntan oil.

'Achtung, achtung... ' the tannoy blares. My husband looks at me. I force a laughed, 'Someone getting a phone call?' but my peace has been assaulted by the rasp of German voices.

Later, that night, there are fireworks. We come at this time to share in the festivities and marvel at the creations of colour and light. This year the bangs seem louder.

*   *   *

We've been here a week. Nothing changes in this magical place. The air is balmy. Crocheting grandmothers still sit in pairs, watching pristine prams, under the shade of magnolia and lime trees decorated with prickly pompoms, the bark looking like an amateur's attempt at painting by numbers. Large marble figures avert their gaze whilst lovers, filled with passion, kiss, make love and share ice-creams next to the burble of fountains. The warm cobbles echo with tantalising scents and sounds of meals prepared to faint operatic arias. We are sitting at the side of the water. I can hear the suck of the waves, as they taste the pink marble rocks edging the lake. I try to translate the euro within my innumerate brain, and calculate our expenses in ice creams. One euro is one ice cream. It's growing late.

We like to swim when the busy throngs are leaving, just before the beach begins to sleep. We wander, hand in hand, to the far end of the lake where the reeds stake their claim for fishy friends and the occasional family of swans or grebes snuggle safely on the shaley shore which is littered with bamboo driftwood and crisp-dried bay leaves. Behind a stone wall, olive trees rest their tired feet in meadowland. There are wild cyclamen under the trees and blue scabious intertwined with pink-throated convolvulus. I peer through a rusty gate, feeling that this must be heaven. A notion comes to me. Perhaps, within my mind, I could make this spot my mother's final resting place. Not the place of stones and skeletons at home. We peel off our outer clothes and immerse ourselves tentatively in the icy water. It takes only seconds of pathetically bobbing up and down, fighting the wake of steamers and speedboats, before we are frozen. We come out laughing, rubbing ourselves with towels still warm from the last of the sun's rays. It is getting late. Soon the beach will be deserted and the preparations for the evening passeggiata will begin. We sit hugging our knees, taking in the wonder of the sunset.

I realise I am happy. I look again at the secret meadow flanked with ancient olive trees and feel the souls of those talented ghosts that live close by. Giotto has loaned his gold to the tired sun which pours it over the wrinkled silken lake. Pisanello and Mantegna offer their reds, pinks and oranges to wash the sky with colour. And as the moon slips behind a cloud to mask its tears, Giulio Romano laughs with life and changes its face to a smile.

I play with the small multi-coloured stones on the edge of the shore and find a piece of nightlight left from a lovers' barbecue. I need to light a candle. An old and valid tradition. I imagine it alight.

I place the little rusty tin on the wall and imagine it glowing and flickering in the darkness. It would gild the dividing wall, the brambles and wild honeysuckle, and would be a symbol of our mutual forgiveness. Every year I will come and light a candle at this rusting fence.

'You're miles away,' my husband says. 'Squeeze in another quick swim?'

THE DAY I MET ELVIS

'Goodness,' said the girl in the supermarket, 'You having a party? Looks like you're going to be doing some baking. You must be good at it. Can I come round?'

Beryl Thorpe laughed with the checkout girl and left with a proud smile tickling the edges of her face.

Next morning, a single black bird jarred the sooty dawn. Beryl slid silently out of bed. Fearful she might disturb Hubert, she crept past the dim mound of his body. She could just distinguish the ellipse of his mouth loosely vibrating, in time with his nasal vibrato. Like an angry wasp in a jam jar. Her tired green dressing gown was still asleep, hung in the corner of the room, her slippers dozing below. As she slid her feet in their rough direction, she banged her big toe on the base of the bed and let out a soundless scream, covering her mouth. Her eyes felt like bulging marbles.

The slippers found, carefully she made her way downstairs. One creak and Hubert would complain for days about being disturbed.

The fridge seemed surprised to see her and muttered a juddering welcome as she assembled butter, flour and eggs and the golden castor sugar that she thought gave a better flavour. She decided not to use the electric mixer, as she wasn't sure how the sound would carry. But she still had two nice coffee cakes, and two cherry, sitting in the oven on number four when Hubert arrived downstairs, with the volume of his aftershave turned up loud.

'What's going on? What's all the mess for? Where's breakfast?'

He sat at his usual place without looking at her. She had laid ready a knife, fork, side-plate, butter knife and linen napkin rolled in a silver ring. He picked up the folded *Financial Times* from the kitchen tablecloth, rattled it as he opened it and swore under his breath at the state of the folding. Then he flicked the remote to get CEEFAX on the television to see how his shares had fared overnight and gazed between them and the paper. She put a steaming smoked haddock on his plate perfectly prepared in milk, and a little butter, as she'd known precisely what time he would be downstairs. It was one of those natural pale things without any additives or colouring. Hubert said that additives made him feel aggressive and moody but Beryl couldn't see much difference in his behaviour.

'So what *is* all this palaver, then?'

'I told you, Hubert. I'm baking for the Bring and Buy at the community centre in the village. It happens every year. You've seen me do it for the past twenty five years.'

116

'Load of do-gooders if you ask me. And who's paying? Be cheaper if you just donated Sainsbury's bill without all this mess.'

'But I enjoy the... ' She looked at him but he never listened. His face had shut down and was immersed again in the paper and figures rolling multicoloured on the screen. He had withdrawn into his polished shell like one of the large snails that climbed the dry stone wall and munched her hostas in the summer. Now and then he put the paper down by his side plate and she watched as he surgically pared the fish flesh from the bones and popped perfect two inch pieces in his mouth. The fish-eating was punctuated by snapped bites of toasted granary bread spread with cholesterol-lowering spread. He looked at his watch and at precisely half past he wiped his lips on the starched napkin, switched off the television, pushed back his seat and moved towards the hall.

'I'm off now,' he said, unhooking his hat from the stand and checking for imaginary specks on the grey pin stripe. 'I'll be home at seven.'

The door slammed emptiness into hollow rooms. When they'd first got married, Beryl had had a new home to make beautiful and there had been that special feeling between them. It warmed lonely times. Now it was as if Hubert's life outside in the business world beat with a more attractive heart. Occasionally he'd get a call in the evening that was work related and she'd hear him joking and laughing – full of charm, enjoying work's sensuous temptations. Then he'd return to his seat either in the lounge with the television or the dining room and his supper, and she'd feel the cold slap of disinterest.

117

But today was different. She had her baking to do. She'd looked forward to it for weeks. All her tapes were planned for day long listening – Elvis with *Heartbreak Hotel* and *Always on my Mind*. She mourned the loss of Elvis Presley, her idol, who died in the same month as their wedding, but played his music and that kept him alive for her. And although they didn't have the same heart-throb appeal, she loved Andy Williams' and Frankie Vaughan's music and decided to end on a lighter note with a compilation of some of their songs.

The day passed pleasantly with a sing-a-long finale of "*You're Nobody till Somebody Loves You*", and "*Give Me the Moonlight*", and a shimmy across the kitchen tiles. 'Daft woman,' she mouthed to the cat, as she embraced a cake tin as a top hat and took a bow by the oven, suitably hot.

By then she'd created two plain Victoria sponges, two sticky ginger, two Devil's Foods, the two coffee and two cherry. As she whipped, beat, folded and cleared, she watched the clock, and just before the final washing- up session, prepared the vegetables for Hubert's dinner. He said that they lost vitamins if they were peeled too early.

There was a click at the door. He was back. She was proud of the cakes cooling on the kitchen tops like fragrant decorations. But he didn't see them.

He walked straight into the lounge where he sat, still in his suit, though he did change into his slippers, a small concession to relaxation. She took in a tray with a pot of tea and the evening paper that he read for precisely half an hour. That gave her time to put the finishing touches to dinner that he liked served in the dining room. She knew she'd be busy that day, so she'd cheated. A tin of Campbells asparagus soup mixed with a dash of milk and a few tinned asparagus made him think she'd been hours preparing the sauce. She'd poured it over some sole fillets that morning – they were baking now – and there were French beans and new potatoes. Melon was an easy starter, and she'd pinched a little of the sponge mixture and poured it over peaches as a sponge pudding.

Before she served supper she washed her hands and face and smeared a quick lipstick outline, no mirror, to show she'd made an effort. When they were first married, he wanted them to dress for dinner. She told him it was pretentious and what would his mother say, and he said it was precisely because of his mother that he set higher standards. In those days she had been more confident – more able to make a stand.

They ate in silence. She tried to make conversation but the words floated away like cartoon bubbles, un-burst.

'How was work?' she asked.

'As usual.'

He ate his supper watching one of his clocks, as if there were programs he had scheduled for the evening, for his sole entertainment. Years ago she said to him that it would be nice if they sat and watched programmes together. But, as he pointed out, their tastes were so different. And she had all day to watch anything she wanted. In the evening, he should be entitled to watch what he enjoyed. After all he'd been working and what did she do with her day? She never suggested it again.

She cleared the dishes as he moved into the lounge and waited for coffee. She saw him slip off his slippers and rest fine-socked feet on the chintz-covered footstool. His jacket was folded carefully and rested on another chair as if he were waiting for a further appointment and was only temporarily in the house. She was exhausted but dare not say so or she'd revive the 'What are you doing it for anyway?' argument.

The ironing nagged at her from upstairs – ten of Hubert's shirts. He'd always considered it common to see washing or ironing on the ground floor. 'Smacks of the washerwoman,' he used to say: a strange turn of phrase coming from him. So a utility room was constructed in the basement of the house and that was where she consorted with the white goods to wash and dry. However she refused to iron down in that spidery dungeon so Hubert agreed to convert a small bedroom upstairs into an ironing room. She dragged her feet up the stairs with the awkward basket on her hip, rested it on the sofa bed made ready for anyone should they wish to stay – fat chance. She switched on the small portable and got involved with Del Boy and his mates, and a Heartbeat video.

Hubert was in bed by the time she'd finished all the shirts. He lay on his back, bulging in striped pyjamas buttoned up to the neck, belly rising and falling in time with the rhythm of his breath. Luckily, she fell asleep almost instantly.

The next day was icing day: that was her favourite – decorating. She even made her own caramel, arranging triangles of the polished dark gold sugar to sit proud on the tops of the Devil's Food cake alternating with triangles of seventy percent bitter chocolate. Finally the cakes were ready. Each cake was set on a pristine white paper doily and then on a good quality paper plate. She wrapped them all in clear-wrap, labelled them, and presented them on a baker's tray she'd bought long ago for the purpose from the cheap ads.

She hid the cakes downstairs overnight in the dungeon as she knew that too much obvious attention bestowed by her on the outside world antagonised Hubert's moods. And he would harp on about the expense, and had she added in the cost of the gas full on for the whole day, the electricity, all those paper plates and wrapping... Supper was the usual strained affair but her excitement bubbled thick through her blood like caramel foaming in the pan.

Mavis came to pick her up at twelve thirty the next day. Beryl didn't drive herself – Hubert never saw the need. She'd put on her best navy pleated skirt and a fresh white blouse and, as she heard the honk of the car, she manoeuvred the tray out of the front door.

'Goodness Beryl! How marvellous. The committee will be impressed.' Mavis opened up the back of the hatchback and the cakes were safely stowed.

'Hop in,' she said.

Beryl sank into the seat watching a drift of sweet and chocolate wrappers float around her ankles. A plastic bottle of water, half drunk, bounced on her polished shoes.

'Sorry,' said Mavis apologetically, leaning across and stashing the bottle into a protesting glove compartment stuffed with receipts, tapes and a woolly hat. 'I don't seem to have the time to... you're so... so organised.'

They arrived at the committee rooms and stood at the back of the hall. For a moment, the noise of so many ladies engaged in convivial chat was deafening. Along the side of the hall was a large trestle table covered with a cloth waiting for the cakes. Beryl walked slowly forward with her baker's tray, feeling the admiration, tasting the unsaid words. She looked quickly at the bounty arranged on the table. Most people had brought one sponge or a few bags of scones or shortbread. As she laid her tray down, Marjorie, the vice-chairman, commented, 'That's wonderful, Beryl. The chairman will be so impressed. I bet you get a special mention.'

She sat with Mavis and some others and the chairman rose to speak. There was a sudden hush. Marjorie gave her a nudge. Just then the door banged open and Fenella Smith glided in, thudding the door behind her. Making extravagant apologies to the chair, she wafted past Beryl, flicking her sleek silvery hair, carrying two large Marks and Spencer food carriers, and, in a very showy manner, deposited her cakes – all boxed, all shop – right next to Beryl's. Beryl watched as the polished silvered nails like sundae spoons arranged the boxes. Then in a voice used to command horses Fenella called out:

'So sorry, Madame Chairman. I know they should be homemade. But I'm sure you'll manage to sell them.'

'Thank you, Fenella. I'm sure we will. It's very generous of you to buy so many for us.'

Warm waves of admiration rippled around the room and Fenella basked in the swell.

'Now. I'm sure you're all dying to buy all these wonderful cakes. Thank you all for your magnificent efforts. I will ask our honoured guest to declare this Silver Anniversary Bring and Buy open. Then we'll all be able to take home these exceptional goodies.'

A spurt of applause followed and the chairman sat down and there was a jostling and a pushing to buy the best cakes. Beryl was too disappointed to look whether hers had gone although she'd never taken one back home yet. She tried to tell herself that it didn't matter. That it was only a cake sale. That there were starving children and homeless people and global warming and important things to get upset about. But she'd looked forward to her moment and now it was stolen.

As she raised her crestfallen head for a moment, she could see Fenella strutting towards her, in beige and gold – cashmere, Beryl thought.

'I could see you looking upset. Sorry she didn't mention yours. I thought they looked very nice – very homemade. I bet they taste delicious. But then you have so much more time for that sort of thing – domestic stuff. My life's so busy.'

Her words razored Beryl. Everyone else was talking, laughing. A turbid blur of sound whooshed round her ears as she sat invisible, wrapped in her cellophane membrane. She didn't notice the salmon quiche lunch or the strawberry trifle for dessert. She needed to leave that place with her baker's tray and run to where it was safe.

Eventually, Mavis was ready to go. She'd had a schooner with lunch and her cheeks were pink. She was awkward as she tried to help Beryl with her tray. At last they got into the car and Beryl dropped into the hollow of the car seat wanting the day to be over. Mavis fired a boisterous farewell to each member through the window. *Come on Mavis I just want to go.* Beryl thought, but said nothing.

Her fingers found a frayed edge. Mavis chatted. She was full of news. 'And did you see Diane's hair? I think that colour's too bright at her age, and I understand the Hewletts are selling up and moving to a cottage in North Wales.' Then she didn't hear the words any more. She had to get home. The nets needed a nice dip with a bit of blue. It was always a job to get them down, washed and back before he returned. And it was four weeks since she'd scrubbed the leaded lights with bleach and a toothbrush. That could be tomorrow. Right now, she'd just got time to tackle the brasses. She had her own method with lemon juice and salt, then a vigorous polish. Then, of course there was Hubert's supper...

Mavis talked incessantly. She rattled on and on about their planned Saga trip to Borneo to visit the orang-utan sanctuary. Beryl would love to have gone. On the other hand it was a long way to see a few apes. When Beryl and Hubert were first married, before the... the sadness, they used to holiday together. Short breaks, to soak up the culture of cities. Hubert specialised in cathedral cities. They did Notre Dame on their honeymoon – all those gruesome carvings of the Slaying of the Innocents. It gave Beryl nightmares and Hubert said she was too sensitive to cope with foreign travel. But they visited Rome and The Vatican, and Toledo – all that silver and gold fashioned into statues, and carved marble figures that seemed almost real. He took endless photographs of churches. Never of her.

Then, after it happened, Hubert said that he needed a few days away on his own, to sort things out in his head. She needed him so badly then with her mother gone and her only sister far away in Manchester. But he insisted. Now he always went away every year for ten days, to a place of cultural value, and she went to Manchester. It was good to see

Iris but Beryl didn't like Manchester very much – all that heavy red brick and Iris's husband made it obvious that she was in the way. Never mind. She usually had one nice day window-shopping and a cup of tea in the Midland, and, if the weather was kind, a day in Tatton Park.

At last Mavis dropped her off. She got the baker's tray out of the boot with much waving and promising to meet soon. Beryl opened the front door to an empty place. She was later than planned with Mavis's chattering and Hubert's supper was in its raw state in the fridge. She ran into the hall and her resoled heels clacked hollow on the terrazzo tiles that twitched with the ticking of Hubert's clocks. But instead of running quickly upstairs to change out of her best clothes and into well-washed older garments, Beryl flopped onto the Jacobean type chair, placed by Hubert as an ornament – not for sitting. *A decorator's chair*, he said, and positioned it at the side of the stairs where it could be admired. It offered no comfort to Beryl. Its stiff horsehair interior resisted her body, telling her to pull herself together at once. She looked around the vestibule, as Hubert insisted on calling it, dabbing tears with a pressed linen handkerchief. Then, gazing down on her shoes, her lace-up shoes gleaming from their extra buff and polish that morning, she recalled Fenella's elegant stilettos and suffered another stab. The ticking of the clocks grew louder and louder. TICK! TICK! TICK! She pushed her hands over her ears to mask the mounting noise. The clocks – Hubert's precious – clocks lived a more privileged life than her. Hubert adored his clocks. Once Beryl had walked around the house counting how many clocks watched her as she worked. Twelve important clocks and as many smaller ticking monsters besides. There were two in the kitchen. One ancient school clock which spied on her with its twelve eyes and its three spiny metal fingers pointing, promising to tell if she broke the rules. How many faces had watched the thing, longing for release from their inky cage into the outside world? Next to that was an ancient timekeeper's clock for clocking in and out in a factory. Hubert thought it was an entertaining piece of history – memorabilia he called it. Beryl saw it as a manacle to shackle folk to a life of intolerable servitude. They had two clocks in the lounge – one a carriage clock from his previous job before he branched out on his own. He'd been allowed to choose. He'd paid extra and managed to get a rare two-train brass cathedral skeleton clock with gothic numerals in a local antique shop. He said it combined his interest in horology with his fascination for cathedrals. His eyes closed with passion as he raved about its six-spoke wheelwork striking half-hourly with a bell and a gong on the hour. Beryl just saw a ghastly thing with its bones exposed, that never kept still and mocked as it counted. On the wall by the fireplace was a French clock, the rays spread out outlined in verdigris. It even had a face painted in the centre. Beryl had longed to kill it. Wipe the smile permanently off its face.

And there was the clock in the hall, a Grandfather clock – rather an ambiguous name considering the circumstances. It was tall and stiff, with a controlling demeanour like Hubert's elderly grandfather. Beryl had met him once before he died. He served in the First World War and would never admit to being even the tiniest bit afraid despite onslaughts of gas in the trenches that reduced his lungs to jelly.

The clock bore a crown of brass balls on its head but Hubert had to clean those himself.

Every other Sunday was clock day. If it was not clock Sunday, then it was car Sunday, when the 1961 Mk11 Jaguar was washed inside and out. Beryl knew the Jag was special. She'd heard about its six-cylinder, in-line water-cooled, twin overhead camshafts, and its three-speed automatic gearbox, and its hypoid bevel rear axle... and its... She'd heard it all. Hubert donned a navy boiler suit that had grown in size over the years, and started by washing the whole car muttering about *Beryl's friends* and what damage bird excrement did to a car and did she have to have a bird table. Once the car was dry, he polished and rubbed until it looked as if it had just been driven out of the showroom. Then it was the mascot's turn to receive his loving fingers, and the grill with special cleaner sent from Jaguar. Then he took out the carpets and shampooed them and hung them over a specially assembled laundry horse that was ready close by. Then he greased all the joints and checked the tyre pressures and the oil, water and windscreen wash. That always made him late for lunch but if Beryl criticised...? Well, she just didn't. But it was difficult to produce a perfect meal with al dente vegetables when time was laughing. After a rushed lunch, he returned to his beloved and spent hours with furniture wax and a cloth polishing the dashboard and the other wooden bits and then he fed the seats... an ironical turn of phrase Beryl thought. At last the car would be finished and returned to the garage and covered for the night with a specially fitted tarpaulin. Once Beryl asked if they could go for a spin when he was finished. After all, it was called a 1961 Jaguar Mk11 3.8 litre *Sports* saloon.

'Go for a spin, go for a spin,' he jeered. 'This car is not for entertainment. It is a tool of work – a business asset – gives people the right impression.'

At least on clock Sunday, she saw Hubert as he worked inside. It began after a vitality breakfast that Hubert consumed in silence with the company of *The Sunday Telegraph*. When finished, he removed her tablecloth from the table and replaced it with Friday's *Financial Times* and two layers of tissue paper so that the print didn't seep. Each clock was lovingly picked off its perch, dismantled if necessary, rubbed and polished with the necessary cleaning equipment which was kept in a navy blue plastic tool box, and when perfectly clean and wound, set back with reverence.

Beryl wished she were a clock that he would want to touch. She wanted him to hold her gently with loving tender hands, slip his fingers over her yielding surfaces, touch her with soft cloths and exotic liquids and set her back on a glorious pedestal once admired.

Eventually she hauled herself from the chair. The cat was kind and rubbed its head against her leg as she made her way into the cellar to deposit the baker's tray. No time to change now. It was Thursday, and on Thursdays Hubert liked fresh chicken breasts grilled with lemon and fresh hollandaise sauce. It was all last minute and Beryl was tired but she knew he expected perfection. A crumble for dessert, that was quick. Just a soft pear from the fruit bowl mixed with a couple of sour plums from the garden and then her instant mixture that she kept ready rubbed in the freezer – his special margarine, a little muscovado sugar, some grated lemon rind and a few porridge oats. She wrapped herself in a large overall saved for emergencies and tried to concentrate on his supper, making plans for the next day, but she relived Fenella and her clever words over and over. Maybe Radio Two was playing songs from the sixties. She caught a snatch of an old Elvis tune and tried to sing along with him. But his song was sad and while he sang about loneliness, he worsened her feelings. But Elvis had galvanised her thoughts. For the first time Beryl looked at her situation objectively. As she moved about the kitchen, she considered her life until that point.

I have to do something so I don't get so upset, she thought. *I have to give my life more purpose. I'm drowning in a conglomeration of velouteed sauces, linen napkins and Italian cotton shirts.*

It was difficult. Hubert checked on everything she did. When she'd tried a flower arranging class, he complained that the flowers were an extra expense, that the pollen on the lilies had stained a good shirt. The voluntary work she tried required her to be away from the house. She couldn't rely on being back in perfect time for Hubert's supper. And it was the relationship with Hubert that she needed to improve.

As he ate his supper, Beryl watched him, trying to distance herself emotionally, assessing him as a naturalist making a film of a rare bird or animal. What would Desmond Morris make of them? It would be easier if she could adopt the impassiveness he showed her. Then they could cohabit like his clocks, animate but without hearts. She watched the way he held his knife and fork, in a slightly affected manner. He wasn't a bad man – he did not stray; well, not to her knowledge. He'd never come in drunk or beaten her and there were stories in the paper every day of such goings on. He had his rules – strict rules – which he liked obeyed. But, nevertheless, their lives ran like trains on divided lines, never meeting except to eat at the same station, and then on disconnected platforms. She knew he believed that everything that had happened was her fault. The doctor told her at the time that was a normal reaction for a man – that he did not know how to cope with blame and therefore would reproach the partner. But it had caused a chasm between them. They were the weatherwoman and weatherman in the gaudy painted present Mavis had brought them from Switzerland. When it rained, he popped out, and when it was dry, she popped out. Welded to their predetermined axes. Never together.

They made their way to bed and, after using the electric toothbrush, the plaque remover, and gargling vociferously, Hubert was asleep in seconds. Nothing stopped him sleeping. But an unjust word in the supermarket, or the bus driver giving her a strange look, was enough to stop Beryl. Tonight Hubert's braying seemed especially loud. Eventually she crawled out of bed, mindful of her feet this time, and sat at the kitchen table with a pottery mug of tea. Hubert disliked mugs, said they were vulgar, and would only drink out of a bone china cup and saucer. But Beryl had one hidden at the back of the cupboard. When she was on her own and need a bit of comfort the old mug came out. She rubbed the cheap glaze with her thumb as she tried to make some sense of her situation.

She heard herself saying *so what?* So what if Hubert didn't see her any more? She was becoming a robot. She was afraid. She was going crazy.

Something must be done, she thought. *There must be a way to make Hubert notice me. To start again – rebuild. So that there is something that matters to us as a couple and my life is not measured in dusters, saved minutes and polished silver napkin rings.*

She re-boiled the kettle to make the tea hot and scalding. Mavis went into town on Fridays. She could go with her. Buy something – a new lipstick perhaps: something to make him notice her. As the idea struck, she was afraid. The norm was indifference, her inexistence. *But if I try to destroy Us as we are, will we be able to cope, restore?*

She banished the doubts, concentrated on the positive and slipped back to the dark next to the stuttering mound of belly, turning and twitching under the sheets.

Hubert seemed to take hours eating his Loch Fyne kipper followed by granary toast spread with sugarless marmalade and two cups of tea. But then suddenly, with his usual bang, he was gone. Beryl's hands shivered as she rang Mavis.

'Come into town with me? Sure, love. You know I always go today. Always delighted. We'll have a coffee in the new place with the easy chairs and the plants.'

This time her feet expected the float of papers in the foot well of the car and they were not disappointed. Mavis was delighted to see her. She made a determined effort to listen to her but... The clouds were steel colanders straining ice rain through measured holes as Mavis parked the car in the car park and they picked their way through black gravel puddles to the platform.

131

Mavis was full of chat. Beryl was glad. It was good to hear someone from the real world.

'See you in a couple of hours,' said Mavis waving a list, as they emerged from the City Centre Station. And she was gone – on a mission. Where to start? Beryl walked slowly with a quaking in her chest, aware that this was no ordinary shopping spree. Oxford Street was a mass of people walking with purpose. Boots would have a lipstick, but no, that was not enough – a lipstick was not life changing.

Now she was outside one of *those* shops. They said that using their products would enhance your marriage. She'd seen documentaries on the television and a group of girls in the committee had a party but she never went. It interfered with Clock Sunday. She turned around to check that no one was watching. Then she looked in the window. The clothes were skimpy, strips and straps and shiny bits with large buckles. Would she have the courage to wear them? They'd make her feel uncomfortable – she was in the wrong place. A group of girls shoved past. Not with any malice; on the contrary, they were giggling and seemed to be teasing one girl who was enjoying the attention. But no. It was not for her.

Her mind revolved around the thought of a new nightdress. Not racy and red or black and covered in fluff and fur, but maybe something elegant. She stopped outside one of the better stores. She'd shopped there for the odd thing: a hat and scarf in the sale years ago. Perhaps just a walk inside for ideas; so she did: past islands of fragrance, up the escalator on to the first floor and into the lingerie department. She shivered as she fingered silks and satins, a blue and green sea; now a garden of soft pastels, pinks, lemons and lilacs. She was spellbound by the colours and the textures of lace and embroideries. Lulled by the warmth and the surroundings.

And then she saw it arranged on a stand. A rich violet nightdress, the colour of passion, in a silken fabric. Delicate straps fell to a fine bodice like a petticoat, decorated with contrasting coffee and lilac lace flowers. She was so entranced that she jumped when an authoritarian female voice boomed from behind.

'It's very chic, isn't it, Madame? Would you like to try it?'

'No... no, it's fine,' she murmured, scrabbling for the price ticket.

'It's a size thirty-six, Madame. I should think it's your size.'

At last she could see the price. It was more than she had ever spent on herself. Beryl was not used to shopping except for apples and cleaning fluids or basic skirts and jumpers.

'I'll... I'll think for a minute,' she stammered.

'Yes, Madame,' said the voice. No doubt she'd seen her type before – the ones that can't spend, that worry about the cost and just finger the merchandise.

Then in a voice that was not hers, from another person within, Beryl said, 'I'll take it.'

Her hands shook as she handed over the banknotes that, until that morning, had sat rolled in a jam jar on the shelf with her homemade pickles. Her emergency, *for a rainy day*, money. She left the store effervescent with excitement and almost ran to the coffee shop.

Mavis looked at the bag when Beryl sat down: studied the label, knew that its silver and burgundy sang of luxury.

'Go on. Let's see, Beryl.'

Beryl pulled out the nightdress and felt its slithery fabric slip through her fingers.

'You dark horse – I never would have thought...'

She sat back with a giggle trapped in her throat.

'Oh it's nothing like that, Hubert has a niece... it's a present. I said I'd get something special.' Beryl smoothed the stitched pleats on her blouse with clammy hands, then slid them down over her wool skirt.

'Very generous if you ask me. Lucky girl. I thought you were going all glam...'

All glam – it hovered round her, a real compliment, the kiss of a butterfly, as they made their way home from the city centre. As she clicked open the front door, she shuffled the phrase through her thoughts, sourcing the queen and the ace, like a pack of cards flicking them over and over. *All glam...* Me... *All Glam*. She tasted the risqué frisson of being that other woman – the one she hoped to be for a night. If the nightdress had that effect on Mavis, then maybe, just maybe... She ran upstairs, slipped the bag in a drawer.

Hubert liked to have a vegetarian meal on Fridays. He said they had richer food at the weekend so that balanced things. Tonight she would cheat. She'd bought some wild mushrooms in the supermarket, so she sautéed them with an onion chopped finely and filled pancakes she'd made in advance. She'd serve them hot topped with a little grated parmesan and a roquette and tomato salad. It would give Hubert the impression that she'd been labouring for hours in the kitchen, and give her, by deceiving him, some satisfaction. He'd begun to buy her the odd fancy food magazine and sometimes pointed with a circular stirring motion as if he was involved with the cooking and his finger had become the spoon.

'Make that,' he'd say. 'I think we'd enjoy that for a change.' It was usually something piled in an elaborate tower as was the fashion – a slice of grilled aubergine on a puree of some vegetable, broccoli or celeriac and then a little grilled steak and a circle of goat's cheese surmounting the lot, or something similar. In the beginning she followed the recipes slavishly, measuring and cutting into fancy shapes, mixing and folding. Then one day, she hadn't had the time. She'd been too long polishing the brasses and she'd put a cloth over the faces of his damn clocks in the kitchen. The radio was playing Elvis, and the comforting tones of his voice slid into the empty crevices of her mind, as soothing as her home-made iced sorbets on a hot summer's day. He was always there in her thoughts, wasn't he?

Suddenly she'd noticed it was getting dark. She pulled off the cloths and it was six forty-five. He'd be home in quarter of an hour. She liquidised frozen peas with a little nutmeg, mint and fromage frais and left that to rest whilst she poured wine and stock into some couscous so it would swell before sitting it in dariole moulds. Then she beat out his precious chicken breasts and rubbed them with a mixture of ground coriander, cumin, a little cinnamon and chilli powder that she set to bake in a hot oven while they went through Hubert's tea ceremony. It was a triumph – her pseudo Moroccan dinner. Hubert was impressed and she'd beaten the clock. It never told. From then on, she decided to cheat using the ingredients that the fashionable chefs employ, the balsamic vinegar, sun dried tomatoes, goat's cheese. Hubert's magazines were full of ingredients that had developed an aura of preciousness about them. Combined and arranged, they initiated the pilgrimage to culinary perfection. For example, at that moment, they coveted the wonders of the sea. In the past, she could only get Hubert to eat salmon or Dover sole. Now, thanks to expensive lunches with clients and the TV chefs, he worshipped at the shrine of cod – soon to become extinct, according to the pundits.

Pancakes sitting in the oven and salad at the ready, Beryl completed Hubert's dessert. She sliced an orange, laid it in a dish then quickly melted a couple of peanut-brittle sweets in a small pan. She drizzled over the mixture and it was ready.

At seven o clock Hubert arrived and hung his coat and hat on the hook in the hall. She knew the number of breaths he made before he sat in the lounge and she counted the same number of steps his feet made on the tiles.

She put on her lipstick and set the table in the dining room.

'Have you had a good day, Hubert?' she said, interlacing her fingers in a silent prayer.

'The usual,' he muttered, already bonded to television and paper. She wanted to tell him about the nightdress, run upstairs, bring it down and pull it out of its fancy wrapping. Twirl in front of him like a dizzy child at her first real party. She wanted to shout, 'Hubert. This is *Us*. We are in danger of losing *Us. You* are in danger of losing *Me*. I am in peril of losing *Me*. I can fall down the waste-disposal of life and get minced away.'

'I'm a bit tired,' she whispered. 'After supper, I think I'll have an early night.'

'Fine,' he said without looking up.

She didn't know how to tell him. How to get him all fired up. She couldn't prise away the screen that closed before his eyes when he looked at her. She'd just have to rely on a fragrant bath and the nightdress.

The dishes washed, she called out 'See you upstairs darling!' But there was no response. So she climbed up the stairs, twenty on the first flight, five on the return. She walked into the bathroom to run the bath. It still had its original black and white tiles, just a few missing, and a white bathroom suite that had always been there. Hubert liked the vastness of an Edwardian bath. It was a devil to keep clean because the enamel was wearing badly. There were mahogany fittings everywhere, a masculine feel to the room. At one time she did try to persuade Hubert to buy some dainty curtains to give the room a little softness, but he had just grumped about women and their blasted fripperies. It wasn't worth the argument.

The nightdress sat waiting for her in the drawer. She pulled it out of the bag with an intense shudder. She had never touched anything so beautiful in her life. It sang of another world. She removed the price tag that was attached by a small gold safety pin. That went into a glass container that sat in front of the mirror. She folded the bag carefully. She would use it as a sewing bag and treasure it. She avoided looking in the mirror. She had misgivings: she could feel the woman from the other side of the glass knocking on the silver, warning her. She wouldn't look. She

137

wouldn't let her speak. Beryl turned away from her and carefully laid the nightdress on her bed.

She had taken the rose water from the kitchen and, as the bath filled, she added some, feeling like an adolescent girl on her first date. The water was warm and soothing and she submerged herself. She tried not to look down at time's insidious attacks. Not to worry, the nightdress would cover the softened flesh on the leg that bore the marks of that fall last year and the broken red veins – the imperfect body of now. In any case, Hubert was not the man she married twenty-five years ago.

Soaking in the water, she considered the best place to sit to catch Hubert's attention. Should she lie in the bed, nightdress on, in a tempting pose? Maybe Hubert would think that a little forward – after all these years and nothing... Surely if he'd wanted to he would have made some kind of advance. It just stopped. Not as a train stops, to carry on again. But a stop – a governing force, like when the hurricane brought down that oak that had grown for centuries and it fell across the entrance to an old path in the woods into her secret place. And no one thought it necessary to remove the carcass. Years of pleasant ambles through scented bluebells and the dank mushroomy days of autumn to pick blackberries and sloes. Finished.

But It finished when she needed comfort, when her body ached with need, the wanting to be with another. He slammed the door to Us. She had heard him in his study, late at night – it sounded like crying. But his door was locked and he wouldn't let her in. As she tapped, hesitantly, his voice, choked and deep in his chest, said Go away! with such vehemence, she was almost afraid. It was a few nights after they were almost three – almost a family. They lost that threeness, that precious expectancy of three. But along with that vanished the closeness of two.

And after that it was as if being with her, being part of her, reminded him of what could have been, and he was afraid of cracking, breaking. People might see a vulnerable side that he had been brought up to think was weak. The rules began: small ones to begin with, silly things that were just not worth discussing. If he wanted to eat supper in the dining room that was fine. If he wanted to spend time on a Sunday seeing to his clocks and that made him contented then that was also fine. But gradually, over the years, the rules increased. Sometimes she felt as if she had become his clock. Embalmed like them, in her case, unable to get out: seeing out, frozen, watching other lives, but incarcerated by time and clockwork.

Had she the courage to change all this? Had she the impudence to suggest that the wearing of a nightdress in a seductive manner after nearly twenty-five years of nothingness would change their lives? The water was chilly. She had lain in the bath so long her skin was crinkled. Not attractive. She dried herself quickly and ran a soft cloth around the surfaces ensuring that all was clean for Hubert's complicated ablutions.

Downstairs Beryl could hear Hubert's TV program – a documentary, or the political stuff he watched, sometimes taking notes. On the odd social occasion when Hubert had asked her to join him she had heard him discuss matters of political interest that she knew he had studied the night before. He made it his business to learn snippets from significant speeches in Parliament, sections out of the newspaper, even Shakespeare. In his life now there was no time for relaxation or laughter. She remembered, just after the bad times, sometimes, a slip of a joke would cross his mind. But in the middle of mirth, he would hesitate guiltily, as if laughter was shameful.

From the landing cupboard she took out her radio-cassette player and an Elvis tape. Hubert wouldn't hear it if she kept the volume low. She went into the bedroom, clicked the tape into the machine, and sat on the bed. Oh, the music. A breath of *Love Me Tender*, and she was smooching in the arms of... was it Richard or Norman? She didn't remember his name. She just recalled her fingers stroking the back of a man's smooth, clean neck, fragrant with something glorious, and strong firm arms that held her tightly – a very long time ago. Being popular, the freedom to laugh without guilt, dressing up and going to parties... all enmeshed in the old music. More and more, she knew, to escape the present, she was dropping into the past. Sometimes the happenings of last week and the week before were difficult to distinguish. Her labours were so routine and monotonous that they merged into a blur of flour and dusters.

Once she'd even been to the doctor to talk about it. She hadn't told Hubert. She sat in a busy waiting room amid babies with runny noses and cruel coughs, stiff and quivering elderly people with sticks and crutches and white and green-faced middle-aged patients who looked worn and tired with disease. The doctor was running twenty minutes late and as she walked in to his consulting room she knew she was a nuisance.

'Well, Mrs Thorpe. How can we help you today?' His head remained down, still engrossed in recording the information from the patient before.

'It's nothing really,' she whispered. Her gaze fell to her reddened hands – there was a spit of pink toothpaste on her cuff. She'd brushed her teeth quickly before she went out. She'd changed, underwear everything and now this damn spit. It looked so unkempt. She pushed the cuff under her navy cardigan sleeve. *I'm not really ill. Was gazing into space, harping back to the old days, an illness?* 'I just... just... feel as if I'm losing my grip.'

'In what way?' he asked, and for a second she saw his tired eyes glance at the small clock squatting on his desk. One of its legs caught her buff record file. It was engraved with some drug company's name.

Tick tock watch the clock.

He was part of the clock people. Far away she heard someone speaking.

'Mrs Thorpe, Mrs Thorpe. Can you hear me?'

'Yes.' He was listening to her chest, through her vest. Then going through the motions of taking her blood pressure.

'Mrs Thorpe.' His voice sounded far away. 'I will tell the nurse to take some blood but I suspect you are just a bit depressed. I can give you something for that, and perhaps a bit of counselling. Come back in a week if you still feel the same and we'll have the results by then.' His eyes lowered: a sign that her allocated time was finished.

She didn't go back. She knew his drugs. She had tasted life in that galaxy. Spinning in the swirling world of slow motion. After the sadness. She had lain on a bed of white sheets with the blood oozing from her body, terrified that she would damage them – despoil, stain with red. She kept crying, *the sheets the sheets!* She could not stop the blood and someone called the doctor – maybe it was Hubert. When the doctor came, she could hear hushed voices in another room. Rubber words with beginnings and endings missing, bouncing around walls. Their meaning indist‐inguishable.

'Drink this,' a voice had said. 'It will do you good, help you to sleep.' A small smooth pellet curved like a white fingernail was forced between her lips with a sticky creamy fluid that glued the sides of her mouth. *Dry... Dry... A drink. Please... a proper drink.* After that she was drowning desperately, hauling herself out of one sea then falling hopelessly into another. And while she was plunging between waters, she could hear Hubert and another world that she could not touch. Her legs were parted and washed by a female voice but she was unable to speak. When she woke, she was in a single bed. There were now two single beds in the room. They never talked about the sadness. She tried occasionally to move into his bed and reach for him but he would turn over and bid her Good Night and she would crawl back into the barren space of her own bed. A few times, over supper, she'd look across to him, slide her hand to try and catch his. But he would brush it away like the nuisance of a bluebottle bumping his panama hat on a hot sunny day, and sink his energies into the newspaper or the clunk of a ball against warm willow on the television.

She'd tried to speak to the doctor then about their situation. But she'd lost her horizontal hold and couldn't express what she wanted to say. 'Hubert is very distant, bitter... shivering ice-cold' The doctor tut tutted.

'Nonsense', he said, 'you've both suffered a terrible shock. He cares for you deeply. Who obtained and paid for the private nurse to care for you? Who ran for your prescriptions'

'But I could have been a sick dog or a cat. I'm a woman, his wife', she said, 'I need... ' She looked at his face, the face of a man she felt was tired of people like her. So she had returned home to the emptiness to fill her days stirring with wooden spoons, and Hubert wound his hours, timed the moments and fed the leather of the car seats.

And now here she was, sat on her bed, twenty-five years later, with a silken violet nightdress in her hands hoping that the garment could reverse their lives. That he would be bewitched by the illusion, forget the past, and she would be his sorceress. It had to be done. She had to halt the downhill slide. There had to be more...

She slipped the sheerness over her shoulders and the straps kissed the tops of her arms. Her belly and back were embraced and the silken fabric slipped gently to her toes. She looked over to the mirror and a far reflection, and for a second smiled approval.

She could hear him on the stairs: twenty up and five across. She must move quickly to the dressing table stool in front of the mirror. The light was soft there and it would be kind to her skin. She glanced up quickly before he walked in, checking her hair, yes greyer, but still soft and curling around her face as it did when they met. Hubert said that he liked her hair... he was coming in. She could feel her whole body shaking with hope.

Oh G-d. Will he be disgusted? I don't think I could cope with his revulsion. No... no. I've made the break. There is no turning back. We need to be two – we are getting older and a lonely future is terrifying. We could be the couple we were. I'll get out the hairbrush. Then it doesn't look so contrived. It's an effort to pull the brush without my hand shaking... She stares at me from the mirror also brushing her hair. But her face looks as if she has decided what will happen.

He walked in. 'I thought you'd be asleep by now. Didn't you say you were tired?'

'Oh yes, Hubert... But I had a pleasant bath and... '

He didn't look at her. She coughed.

'Is there something you want? You've been very strange this evening.' Irritation ground his voice. He pushed through the gap between Beryl in her violet nightdress and the bed, and, taking his striped cotton pyjamas with him, stomped into the bathroom.

Maybe he didn't see me properly. His bed preparations are so much part of his personal routine that perhaps I should wait until he returns. Looking at me in the mirror. Is she smirking at me? Has she watched my actions, seen the nightdress, been witness to my sorcery? Smelt my desperation?

Hubert came out of the bathroom buttoned up to the neck, grey hair slicked into a wet smooth cap. He looked at Beryl with puzzlement. Her glance fell down onto her legs covered with the silken fabric. He walked slowly as if his thoughts were disarranged and he'd shuffled them in his mind, until they were tidy. Then he leaned over her shoulder talking to her reflection. 'Are you sure you're all right? You're not having problems with your age or something? I know women... of well... they can feel a bit strange?'

'No Hubert, I am fine. I just wanted to... to try.'

144

But Hubert had picked up a magazine. He always allocated half an hour for reading before he retired.

She shuddered. The mirror snorted, *I told you so.* Beryl moved in front of its carved frame and the image bent with a fun-fair twist.

I'm in a house of mirrors and they are contorting in time to the tick of the clock. I no longer exist. I am desolate. I had hoped... Would it be worth trying again tomorrow? No, I am beaten. Hexed by the mocking mirror and the ticking clocks. Time has taken Hubert. And there is my pride. A small animal sitting on my shoulder burrowing in my mind with powerful paws and strong nibbling teeth, forcing me to think of myself. Stupid girl.

Beryl had never felt so isolated– so dead. Hopes of a new bright future had been concentrated in the purchase of a silly nightdress. How could that possibly change a routine that was so set that it was now practice? All that remained was the possibility of living with someone who had become a stranger. Sharing his space, but never his soul.

She peeled off the nightdress and folded it, feeling bereft of the softness, suddenly cold, putting it carefully in a drawer. The mirror watched as she replaced it with the usual pale-blue brushed cotton with its lace collar and small pin-tucks.

It eyed her: *told you so.*

The first of the birds – the blackbird that sat at the uppermost top of the chestnut tree – shattered the silence and began his early morning sonata. Beryl avoided the evil-eyed clock with its pointing fingers and turned to look across at Hubert. She knew she still felt affection for him despite everything. He was much quieter now. Heavy snoring had given way to a softer sound and as his face fell towards the shadows Beryl could see the blurry image of the man she married. Another hour passed and the grey dusk was lightened. Ribs of light seeped through the sides of the curtains. Beryl heard the clatter of the milkman's crates and the electric drone of his float mixed with starts of the first cars. Other people moving through their lives.

She'd make an early start. She dressed quietly with her head heavy with night thoughts. She walked downstairs with the creaks of the house acknowledging her arrival: through to the kitchen and the cat stretched in its basket smelling of night sleep and fishy feasts. She bent down to her, back creaking.

What am I going to do, Button? I know I have to stay, I have no money of my own and at my age I'm virtually unemployable, can't use a computer and anyway, I still love Hubert. I just want us to change. I don't want to go. But I am afraid, so afraid of losing myself.

She put on some porridge and automatically cut a small fruit salad to accompany the porridge. Then she set the percolator to brew some fresh coffee. The aroma of freshly ground coffee out of the sealed tin was wonderful. Hubert was not keen on fresh coffee in the week as it encouraged his arthritis. Cup brewed, she took her coffee, cauldron black, and sat by the window. A gaggle of magpies was fighting over a black bag they had managed to spike. Damn, that was a job she'd have to do later, clean up the old tea bags and the apple peelings and Hubert's shredded notes. The paper thudded through the door and absentmindedly she glanced at the date. The seventh of February – a week to go to St Valentine's Day. No, she didn't expect, hadn't considered, receiving a Valentine for years. Hubert said that it was just another excuse for merchandising. But traditionally, it was supposed to be the day that the birds paired and...

It was different when they married in August seventy-seven. When Elvis Presley died. He was desperately unhappy and lonely too. Poor fellow. Some of the girls at work were so distraught they stayed away for a few days. She was too wrapped up in Hubert and the wedding to worry. She had the picture of the two of them downstairs in a silver frame. She wore a guipure lace dress her mother made in a Victorian style with a frilled collar and leg of mutton sleeves.

She remembered, draining the coffee to last drop, how she and Hubert were happy, full of fun – in love. She teased him because he was always a bit of a snob and was unhappy in their flat near her Mum and Dad. He couldn't wait to move and get *on the right side of the tracks*, as he put it. Beryl loved it. She could pop home and have a laugh and she didn't feel lonely. He was already so ambitious: making appointments to see clients late at night. Never satisfied: working harder and harder, ambitious for more, to prove to the world that he was a successful man.

He was so determined that his child would be born at a good address. When she was eight months pregnant they moved to Kington Chase. Even now she could feel the tearing agonising pain as she tried to move one of the packing cases.

She could hear Hubert stirring upstairs. She would reheat his porridge, make some toast.

'Good morning, Hubert,'

'Morning,' he muttered, unfolding the paper and reaching for the spoon, in a synchronised movement that also involved his wristwatch. His eyes returned trance-like to the television screen. Nothing had changed in him. Everything was the same. Last night when she tried to water their lives into life, it was impossible because there was only dead soil.

She must clear the bin bags before he saw the mess. The dining room furniture needed a good polish. Button's bed was desperate for a good scrub with disinfectant. But it was Saturday and she would try to rest a little, for tomorrow was clock Sunday.

Thank goodness for Monday. Clock Sunday passed. Supermarket today. Her body was present but her mind lurched like a hunted fox. She woke to a fine day heavy with birdsong and clear blue skies. *Nice to see some bright weather at last,* she said to the bus driver. He wasn't used to people speaking to him but he acknowledged her comments with a grunt that she interpreted as *yes.* She made herself touch the chrome bar that edged along the seats so that she knew she wasn't dreaming. Underneath her legs, the prickly velvet fabric talked to her. She trailed her index finger along the design in a kind of dance to music beating in her head. What was that tune called? It repeated and repeated, like a stuck record.

The bus listed forward to the stop by the supermarket and she released her hold on the prickly fabric and swayed towards the front, as she knew the driver would not wait. Hubert had bought her a rather ingenious fold up trolley that was made out of a fine material like umbrella fabric. He'd found it in a catalogue in one of his Sunday papers.

She opened the bag and made her way into the fairground of food where music always played. A carousel of consumption. She'd looked forward to today. Sometimes she saw an acquaintance and she usually had a cup of coffee when she'd finished. Really it was an outing. Last time she came it had been when she bought all the cake ingredients and the young girl at the checkout was so friendly. She still ached with that stupid loss though she knew it was nothing. But there was no joy today. Just monotony as she pushed her trolley, careful not to touch anyone, watching the prices and the date stamps – *you can't be too careful. They always put the old stuff in the front so it's used up first. Buy what's in season, but these days it's hard to know what's in season. Remember when we were young and February meant the first tiny forced shoots of rhubarb – they cost a bit more but mixed with some stem ginger and a little sugar, they made a wonderful tart or crumble.* Then there were the Seville oranges. Beryl enjoyed making marmalade. But Hubert decided to use the sugar-free stuff to cut down on calories. She thought he resented her pleasure in placing the waxed discs onto the firming golden mixture. Jars labelled with her own name and cellophane pulled tight as a little see-through hat. Well, those days were gone, and the days of homemade jam for the same reason. *Concentrate Beryl.* Canary tomatoes were on special offer. They'd make a tasty salad. Did she need window-cleaning spray, bathroom spray, cat food?

The whole place was blurry. Everyone was wrapped in cellophane and the carousel of food turned faster and faster. She rested for a moment against the trolley, glad of its heaviness. Of course she didn't get any sleep again that night and she couldn't face any food that morning. Her head was dropping down. There was a voice close to her.

'Are you all right Madam? Would you like a glass of water?'

'Yes. Yes, that would be kind.'

Suddenly a chair was under Beryl's bending legs and a glass with cool water rested against her lips.

'Take a sip, love, come on now. Are you on your own? Have you anybody with you?'

She heard the questions through a fog of faintness. Oh the embarrassment. *Stupid woman. Fancy going without food: such a fuss over nothing. What would Hubert say?*

'I'm fine now, honestly,' she said, suddenly realising there was a crowd around her chair. 'Really I'm all right.'

'Is there someone we can phone?' A young lady glanced at her ring. 'Your husband perhaps?'

'Oh no, please don't call him.'

They walked her to the restaurant and she was given tea and biscuits and a supervisor talked to her. They chatted about the weather and her last big shop with the baking supplies and then she looked at Beryl's loaded shopping trolley.

'I'll get Mike to help you with that,' she said. 'I'll get him to wait with you and see you on the bus.'

The dizziness was clearing and through the mists a young man came towards her. His shirt collar was pushed up about his neck. His hair was pulled back into a black greased creation and a slick fell forward loose into his eyes whilst his trousers were drainpipe tight.

'Elvis!' Beryl gasped.

'That's right, darling. I'm Elvis. Mrs Stanley has asked me to see you onto the bus, as she's a bit worried about you.'

She followed the young man out of the store and he hummed a gentle tune under his breath. That familiar velveteen vibrato. She'd heard that special voice so many times before. At last he'd come to her when she needed him. Now she would never be alone. She watched as he swaggered ahead of her.

Yes. It was the way *he* walked. All hips and action. Her heart jumped.

'You just ask for me next week, darling. I'm just here to look after you.'

Her bus arrived and he lifted the shopping onto the bus with strong young arms.

'Don't forget darling', he said. 'I'll see you next week. I'll look out for you. OK?'

CHRISTMAS CHEER

I bought the ingredients for the Christmas cake today. I can't believe it's another year gone. I used to enjoy this point in the calendar – the run up to Christmas with festive lights all a-glitter, the carol services, hot mince pies, the hustle and bustle and that burgeoning something that makes me feel young again, a kiss of childhood.

Jennifer and I used to go to London to look at the store windows together. We'd start at Fortnum's, look quickly at Browns, then into Regent Street to finish with Liberty's and Hamleys. We'd reminisce about the stuffed toy elephants dressed as sugar plum fairies in Hamleys and Liberty's amazing bronze figures that looked as if they had stepped out of an Erte picture.

I'm late this year with the cake. Usually I start in the middle of November, bake it and leave it in the dining room wrapped in layers of greaseproof paper and silver foil, giving it a good dose of brandy at the beginning of December and waiting for it to settle before icing. Otherwise the brandy can leach into the icing and spoil the final effect. I prefer to cover it in white marzipan – I think the yellow is so common and I still make my own royal icing. I dislike that fondant stuff so beloved of Jane Asher and her disciples.

Jennifer used to help me in the past. We made quite an occasion of it, stirring and wishing, and Edward used to say that the wishing made it taste better. This year, Jennifer will be with her husband and his family. The boy was not our choice, of course, and I said to her when we were laying the Sunday lunch at about this time last year, 'Jennifer, you realise that this liaison is for life, not just a whim like the time you had to have that rabbit and I was left to care for it all through your university life'. She laughed, tears running down her face. Then her face contorted and she said, rather bitterly, I thought, bunching her shoulders and sniffing, 'No. Jacob is not a whim.'

I remember the first time she brought him to the house. She hadn't mentioned that he was different. Well, he is good looking in an obvious kind of way... some would say Mediterranean, some might say swarthy. Yes, tanned with good teeth. 'You make him sound like a horse,' she said. I didn't take too much notice in the beginning; she's had lots of lads through the house. But then, on that Friday, she runs in the lounge all flushed. I was having a WI meeting and was just offering a cup of tea to Mrs Hopkins in the best Royal Albert, Country Roses, when she burst in.

'Where's Dad?' she says. 'Jacob wants to speak to him.'

Edward was impressed. But secretly my heart turned over. Well, they're just not the same as us are they? Yes, he bought her a lovely engagement ring and the parents were very pleasant... too nice, almost. We asked them over to discuss the wedding arrangements. I'd always planned the local church and a little marquee at the side of the house with a laid buffet... a whole ham, turkey and some good prawns. There's a wonderful picture in a recipe book where the prawns cascade pink and tempting... a kind of fishy fountain. But the food was not acceptable and the church...

Mr Samuels kissed me when we met. And when we sat down he explained that Jennifer had decided to take lessons so that she and Jacob could marry in the synagogue. Then, after, they wanted a meal at the Hotel Ambassador and he was happy to pay because some of his guests would require a kosher meal. Did he think we couldn't manage to pay?

It was a terrible shock. I have nothing against that type. I have Jewish friends myself... good friends. It's just having them in the family...

Jennifer took her lessons very seriously and in the spring they were married. The synagogue is not very different from our church in layout and Jennifer walked down the aisle with her father, but there was a little ceremony first when Jacob had to go to the back and lift her veil to check that she was the right one. Actually I thought that was quite sweet. They stood under a prayer canopy with the Samuels on the one side and Edward and myself on the other and there was a choir and an organ the same as us but they had a "cantor" who sang most of the service. My Jennifer looked beautiful, of course, and the synagogue was fragrant with masses of white lilac, freesias and carnations in soft pastel colours. At the end of the service, Jacob stamped on a glass and there was a lot of kissing.

Then after, in the hotel, Jennifer and Jacob were sat on chairs, raised shoulder height and danced around the room. It was very noisy but it's traditional, I suppose. The food never stopped – five courses. Different wines with dinner and champagne for a toast at the end. Mr Samuels sat himself next to me. 'Nice to see them so happy,' he said. I thought she, Mrs Samuels, was overdressed, flashy with her long dress and her cocktail hat and her high heels. I told Jennifer before. 'I don't want anything fancy.' She wanted us to go up to London and get an outfit for me but I wouldn't have it. I told her that last year's beige from Uncle Angus's eightieth would do fine. It wasn't a celebration for me, after all.

After the honeymoon they came round with some perfume and a bottle for Edward, quite unnecessary.

She says they don't have a tree or decorations at Christmas but they celebrate Chanukah. She asked us to go up there but...

It's a large cake for Edward and I to manage.

SLIPPING THE SKIN

With only a hospital gown to protect me, I slide my bare foot from the shiny lino onto the scales of ice metal. My judge. I feel those other eyes, the forty fascinated, pitying orbs of the Hospital Slimming Club, pressing into the space between my shoulders and through my head. Sister Felicity pushes the marker up, up, up like the blade of a guillotine.

I look at her and my face pleads 'whisper.' She drops the block and shouts out the verdict with a sergeant major's bark; I shrink into my layers, my condemned cell of fat. Though I've smiled and pretended to laugh.

Head lowered, trying to escape the murmur of tongues, I return to my locker and pick up my clothes, discarded to save an ounce of poundage. Sensible shoes, navy brogues with laces that can bear my weight bought out of the Sunday newspaper, a navy button thro' dress. I thought the buttons looked slimming when I first wore it. Now, rather than hold the thing together, they seem to conspire to pop at embarrassing moments. A wooden bangle from India, well, from Oxfam from India, carved with elephants – a present from Aunty Maud – and a necklace of glass rainbows that I found in a junk shop which looks like diamonds when the sun catches its prisms.

I walk home alone. The bus never seems to come along our route and the drizzle shifts into the gap between my coat and neck. Shuddering with cold, I slide the key into the lock. My skin is damp like a dog's chill coat. I am thinking only of what to eat, to squash her voice: perfect Sister Felicity in the size ten uniform, starch-stiff with the cinched elastic waist, like there's no body inside.

Shall I have a bowl of Jordan's crunch with warm milk or creamy mashed potatoes and peas with some golden fish fingers, or just a large tin of rice pudding warmed in the microwave with a tin of peaches... or just chips?

But I have a hot bath first to erase her wounding. A cleansing of Sister Felicity.

Gran has baby-sat so I can have the evening, and my little brothers and sisters are now asleep in bed. The house shifts from leg to leg, creaking occasionally. There is a faint smell of perspiration as I peel off my clothes again, so I toss everything into the clothes-basket.

The bath is good. It is hot... but it is small and I am... larger than I wish. I try to forget that the water will not reach any part of me unless I hang one leg outside or press both legs flat against the base of the bath so there is space for it to flow. Lying down with the warmth and vaporous scent of soft green forests drifting around me, I try to convince myself that Sister Felicity doesn't matter. That I will lose the weight and that her tone of condemnation cannot hurt me. But the memory of it unpicks my quiet.

It's difficult to get out – I tend to stick to the bottom – but I manage it with a few more bruises and balance precariously on the side of the bath. Her words are now a snake's hiss:

If you don't lose weight you'll be dead.

I take the towel – it's brown, worn with shaggy bits and I hate it. But it's all I have right now. I pull its rough surface onto me and try to wrap it around. It knows me intimately, never tells of my secret folds, my private flaps of body.

I'm tired from the effort and the day and I try to chase the trifles and the puddings from my thoughts even though my stomach is contracting with hunger because I starve on the day of the weighing. I take my nightdress that is folded under my pillow, pull the old gold brocade curtains tight into a seam, and fall into bed.

My room is cold. The bed is ice. I drop into its dipped centre. There is a shiver in my body but the darkness is comforting. It cannot see me. It does not want to look and it never judges.

My door creaks open. I screw up my eyes and see my father's body silhouetted, in underpants and string vest, a cigarette in his hand. I can distinguish the red stab of light as he moves into my dark, taking a puff, filling my room with acrid smoke. He shuts the door and there is only that red light and the smell in my blackness. I close my eyes even though they need to watch what he will do and I pretend to turn over in my sleep, press my curves and folds against the wall so that there is no space for his hands and his...

I feel the pad pad of his bare feet across the shiny lino. He leans over me, so close I can hear his breath and mine in tune.

Suddenly the bed bends with weight, and cigarette smoke hangs heavy over the creaking. 'Shh,' he mutters. 'Don't wake the little ones.'

It is later, much later and I trudge to the bath again. I need to wash away his fingers and his smell. The tears will not come and I lie there, scrubbing the sticky mess trying to imagine the soft loving muzzle of that Labrador I met in the park, and bright red poppies and the sun and another world. And I dream of slipping the skin, of moving out of my monster cage of flesh to a clean, slim, beautiful world.

Soon I am cold. I manage to pull myself out. But I am tired and I cannot fight him and Sister Felicity. I crawl downstairs, pulse racing. I open the box of magic tricks – the goodies cupboard – and pull out the little ones' fondant fancies dressed in their pink and chocolate party-dress icing. I push them in my mouth, then a box of orange cup cakes and I wash it all down with coke and I feel sick. I cram sticky golden popcorn out of a large rustling packet into my mouth with two fists but there is no picture show. Then I make up a pint of butterscotch custard and slice in some bananas. My hands are shaking and my heart is tap-dancing to the same music. But the crying beast inside is silent now and I will sleep. I fall into bed with the voice of Sister Felicity and the sick smell of smoke in my bedclothes and promise *tomorrow I will start.*

In the morning, I dress the little ones; help them with their school clothes.

'Don't forget your sandwiches. Have a lovely day,'

The bus picks them up. They climb on happy and I return to the kitchen, make a pot of tea, not able to eat with the fullness of everything choking in my throat. He sits there with his pressed clean suit, ready for work smelling of aftershave, playing with his mobile phone. He does not speak to me.

Then the house is empty. It gives me time to think. *This cannot go on.*

I phone the doctor and ask the receptionist for an appointment.

'Yes doctor can see you. In eight days... unless it is an emergency...'

'No, no. I say... I can manage.'

So I make my shopping list. Then remove the dressing gown that is my friend, kind and soft, and put on clothes that hurt. I can't find tights that fit. Even the largest size split straight away. So I go barelegged even in the winter, unless I don men's joggers from the outsize shop. Those will do today with a man's baseball cap and trainers. I have to push the pram slowly because my legs are chafed and sore. As I walk down the street, I feel stares. Eyes bounce over the undulating rolls of flesh on my back, around my arm flaps and fall over the creases in my legs. I am lucky that the pram hides my extra stomachs in the front.

We arrive at the supermarket. Walking up and down the aisles is safe, clean – a hallowed place with flowers and smiles. I follow the psalms that chorus through the loudspeaker. I hear the chants of supervisors:

'Can you help to pack here please? Can you help with this customer?'

'Can I stay where it is warm and friendly?'

'And Gala apples are on special, two bags for the price of one.'

I buy four. We leave the safe never-never holy land of hermetically-sealed food packets that are clean, undefiled. I push the pram back to the dark house at the end of the street because the baby needs her sleep and now there is no one to talk to except the food. As I unpack, it chants its own anthem:

'And slices of bread white squashy bread
With butter and honey and thick chocolate spread.'

The children return with a bang of the door, a cacophony of noise, a whirl of dirty clothes and pictures drawn of men with stalk fingers and wide smiles that are labelled Daddy. My dressing gown hangs waiting. It welcomes me with its softness, and after tea and bathing and stories, I crawl to bed. He will not come tonight. He is away. I am safe. *But this cannot go on.*

Felicity is a serpent. Felicity is a snake. She stabs me with her forked tongue; her sinuous hips shimmy like a snake, a diamond back, viperous, slipping and sliding. I wish I were a snake. I want to be a snake. If I were a snake I could slip away from his fingers.

Downstairs beckons with its sultry voice. It seduces me with its night call – the neon strum of the fridge.

'Come taste, come taste my packets, I have a whole trifle and Brie

Luscious to lick, spread on the toast, waiting for you with the tea.'

I need it to fill my emptiness. When I am eating I am safe from the fingers, safe from Felicity and her army of eyes and murmuring mouths.

I drag my body out of bed promising only to eat celery sticks and carrots. The clock ticks mockingly as it watches me move into the kitchen. I sit at the table. The fridge hums contralto that I can be its mistress – it knows my routine. I press my thudding temples with plump fingers. A pulse thrums through my body and I think of the serpent. I think of Felicity, and I get up. *This can't go on.* I will go back to bed with the pain of no. The fridge beats out a syncopated rhythm as it shouts after me. It shows me its sheeny legs encased in stockings and suspenders and I ignore it. The larder whispers as I pass. I take an apple from the crystal fruit dish in the hall and I trudge back to bed with the fight in my mind. I want to be a serpent like Felicity.

And I fall asleep. A tired moon dipped in smoke sits low over a peak of nougat and Madeira rocks. There are outcrops of sparkling caramel crystals filled with chasms of sticky rice pudding. I must reach the summit to escape from Felicity. But she is close. As I puff with the steepness of the ascent, having to eat as I go, my legs grow heavy. My feet and ankles become ensnared in a viscous liquid. Threads of melted sugar spin themselves about my body. But I force myself on – a hounded animal with the sound of the chase in my ears. At last I am at the peak, reaching through blue skies. Down below me, deep valleys shelter misty orchards.

Then I hear the hiss of Felicity advancing, very close, feel the movement of air from her forked tongue and I try to run down the mountain. But my feet are stuck to a rock. As I pull, something within me snaps and my body lengthens and lengthens. I'm writhing and extending, curving down. My feet melt and disappear. I turn around. Open my jaws till they disconnect; engulf Felicity and slither my way to my garden with the finest red apples. There I sleep.

*   *   *

The morning sky is a bright blue tent. I dress the children.

'Don't forget your sandwiches. Here's the money for the school trip. Straight home after OK? or I'll worry.'

Now it's just the baby and me. So we go to the park to play on the swings. I'm pushing her up high so her laughs fall on my shoulders like peals of crystal bells. She knows no fears. Inside I hear the serpent's voice urging me.

You can break the circle of bruises and eating. NOW!

The swing beats back and fore and its rhythms shout: *THIS WON'T GO ON!*

Shall I get a lock fixed? But he will be angry and there will be more pain. Thoughts whirl around my mind as we return. *A ring a ring a roses*, and I give the baby her boiled egg with soldiers and put her in her cot for her afternoon rest.

*   *   *

The house sleeps. I know there is little time. In the blue light of the sitting room the late night news mutters stories of bombs, floods and starvation. I go down, take two of the bags of apples and return to my room, sliding the wooden frame of the chair under the round knob of the door. It is sealed: locked without a lock. I have considered this many times but I have never had the courage until today. Now my room is a safe space, a haven. I empty one bag of apples into a bowl – the glass punch bowl we use at Christmas – and place it on the bedroom window-sill. Then I take another bag and lie on the bed. My private bed. I empty the bag of apples over my body and slide my fingers between them so they become ornaments: vast jewels of garnet red striped with pink. Three rest on one hand, another two about my neck. The curtains are open to the night and the silent velvet watches. I sit back against my pillows and eat one apple, relishing the crunch, licking the juice that runs down my fingers.

Then I shiver as a rhythmic tapping drums at the door. The old routine – our comedy of manners. Muffled sounds of pleading words and a hint of acrid smoke. A knife of light that holds his shadow gashes through the dark. I close my eyes, calm my shaking and drown his whispers with the munching.

I have tasted the fruit. Now I can stop the bruises. I can peel away the past: slough off my casing. I possess the power.

I *will* be a snake like Sister Felicity.

THE DOG'S BLANKET

What constitutes infidelity? Two hands touching like the brush of a lace-wing, as they reach for a phone? A walk in the park together, oblivious to the world? Or a look, an exchange of glances that goes beyond starriness to a deeper constellation? And why suddenly turn from a life that seemed good (well averagely good) and follow temptation? What is the trigger that banishes loyalty and suddenly exclaims, 'Why not!'?

I thought I'd been enjoying my life at home with a husband and two children. Time had moved on and the children could look after themselves if they had a day off school, so it was my moment to break free and return to the job market. I wanted a job with variety. I could type but wanted to escape that life, so I'd started working for a small paper and sold advertising space.

I've tried to think why it happened. Matthew and I were happy with each other – we never rowed. Well, not major rows. There was the odd niggle if he forgot the wine on the way for our dinner party, or arrived home two hours late because he had to keep some of his boys in and didn't think of ringing and I'd made something special and was playing the oven game moving things up and down – a barn dance with the shelves. But there was nothing major. Sex was still good though less frequent. He was a considerate lover and I never felt rejected. But maybe after fifteen years of pushing the same buttons and pulling adequate stops, there wasn't that spontaneous got-to-do-it-now feeling. Sex had to fit in with timetables, when the kids weren't in the house. A routine, maybe, like going to Sainsbury's early on Monday to miss the rush, or filling up with petrol before the weekend.

I did try to speak to him about it. I tried to offer tentative discussions because we never did talk, not in detail, like we talked over the new shed or the summer holidays. I suggested we took the old blanket and a picnic, took a trip up the Abergavenny Canal as we had in the old days when we'd moor the day-boat after a while and walk hand in hand in the forest.

I kissed his ear. 'It's years, love, since you laid me down on the blanket in the midst of pearl-white anemones, banks of moist moss and made love to me with the fragrance of blue bells scenting our movements. It didn't matter that branches were digging into me through the blanket. Remember our bodies gasping, and we'd scream with the passion of it… it was exciting… it was unpredictable… and it was you and me.'

Matthew turned to me in horror, as if those people hadn't been us but some others that he'd read about in his paper and then tsk tsked under his breath.

Matthew was very conscious of his position as the deputy head, wanting and hoping to be head in five years. That spontaneity and passion had been washed away in a flood of school reports, marking, and a mound of sardine paste and cheese and pickle sandwiches.

'It's too risky,' he scorned.

'But we're married. So what if there was a headline in the Western Mail or the Penarth Times, that Matthew Thomas and his wife were caught inflagrante, in the woods near Abergavenny?' But he snapped his face, formed his mouth into a letterbox, and gave me a look as if I was a sixth-former caught smoking in the toilets. I only suggested it once.

Another time just before Christmas, after a day's shopping, I felt a closeness helped by a couple of glasses of red. I whispered to him that I might dress up as a tart and sit in a hotel bar, and that he could pick me up and take me back to his room. But there was that face again. So I gathered up my fantasies, popped them in the loft of my mind – well, tried to – and made do with long walks in the park looking at others and pretending not to see.

So we muddled on, happy enough. He became more involved with his job and the government inspections that terrorised our lives before they happened and the elation when all had gone well. It was simply the way we lived. But the school was in a good catchment area, the children's parents were motivated and he spent so much free time there that I'd have been surprised if all was not well.

But then it happened. It was waiting in the wings of my life. I suppose I felt like an understudy with that starring role just out of reach. The office decided that they would do a regular feature on antiques that would appeal to their AB readership and it was up to me to try and rustle up the advertising. I'd scanned Yellow Pages and planned my campaign but many of the antique shops were closed and those dealers I'd managed to see were either suspicious, thinking I was from the police or trading standards, or just gruff and uninterested. So when, on my last visit of the day, I pushed through the stacked frames and dusty chairs and tables, waiting to be attended to 'out the back', I was surprised when a tall middle-aged guy, late forties with a crinkled face, smiled at me and asked how he could help.

'I'm from the Penarth Mirror,' I said, offering my card and unnerved by his bright, blue-eyed stare. He understood that it was advertising and, yes, he might be interested and, give him a few minutes to get the waxes off his hands, and we'd go for a coffee to discuss details. His name was Jed. I looked in his eyes and something was triggered in a lonely space. Those emotions that I'd so tidily wrapped up were forcing their way out. I tried to convince myself that I was just excited, that after a grey wet day when the predominant answer had been no, someone was interested in doing some business. And if he was pleasant-looking, it made my job easier. But my frustration had been simmering for years. I stood at the back of the shop listening to running water and ignoring the querulous voice of my maiden aunt who sat on my shoulder and stabbed my conscience. Jed, even in worn beige chinos and an old blue sweater, looked so good. We walked to a small coffee shop and sat in the corner, I tried to concentrate on my business patter and admired the turquoise and lilac décor and the bleached wood floor and the single orange gerberas arranged in sandblasted glass vases.

'It's very pleasant in here,' I murmured. Pathetic platitudes.

'Yes,' he said, crinkling his eyes, and mouth dancing with humour. I laid out my papers to show him the rates for full, half page etc.

'Yes,' he said, his eyes fixed on my face and totally ignoring my spiel, 'whatever it costs, I'll do it. But you must sort out the layout. I don't want any pimply adolescent coming round to finish the thing. And if I give you a series of half pages, then you must come with the copy each time.'

I nodded, heart pounding, thinking that there would be at least five more occasions when I would see him. I had to steady myself before I could climb into my car with a modicum of decorum. Damn it! I was kidding myself that this was work. My thoughts were no better than all these men 'playing away' that I'd ridiculed in the past. It was dark by the time I got home. But there was nothing to blame myself for; a little flirtation with my eyes, maybe.

Matthew was angry. He said he was worried and that I always rang when I would be late. He wanted to get on with a report but the children – fourteen and thirteen – had cornered him. They had heard about this giant Schnauser puppy for sale. We had promised them a dog on Alex's fourteenth birthday and that was in three weeks time. I'd been thinking more of a Westie or even a rescue greyhound. But the two boys, and even Matthew, ruled me out.

'They're women's dogs,' they chorused.

'But it still has to be manageable,' I argued. But my voice was lost. Here was the chance to get this oversized animal and the winter holidays would be a good time for them to get to know each other.

'And Mum. You promised. You said that if we got up every day before school and walked it, then popped in lunchtime –'

I saw a very large animated noose in front of me. This animal would ultimately be my responsibility. I was angry. I looked at Mathew's expression and was dismayed to see a light of triumph. Perhaps he'd even like it if I had to give up work.

The next day, after a trek to Petsmart for a collar and lead and worming tablets, and a toy and basket, the puppy arrived. It already seemed the size of a large dog – a tangle of pepper and salt fur and bright blue eyes that glinted with devilment.

'It needs something nice and soft to put into the basket,' shouted Mickie wildly.

Matthew had caught the children's enthusiasm. 'There must be an old rug or something in the airing cupboard for him – something snugly.' He rushed upstairs to root in the depths of the airing cupboard. After dragging out an old electric blanket that was too good to throw away, and a pile of grey towels bought by mistake in the sales, he found our rug. Yes, our rug, safely put away for sentiment, for me to get out now and then and remember sweet times. It was wrapped in a bag with a few of the children's first babygros.

Don't be pathetic, I told myself. It's a rug. It's a tatty tartan thing – well past its life. But I still felt betrayed. He was able to discard our rug – and give our past – to a puppy who happily spent the next hour shredding the damn thing. So in the end, we had to use the grey towels in his bed. The whole incident was ridiculous and maybe it was just hormones but I was

172

devastated. And now I could feel Jed's eyes, and feel the wanting like it used to be.

I'd arranged to meet Jed as soon as the layout was sorted. 'He's a special client,' I muttered in the office. 'Went for a series of six half pages straight away.' I tried to look casual pretending it was business, but when I picked up the phone to make the appointment to see Jed, my heart was thudding in my chest.

'Great,' Jed said warmly. 'Let's do it over dinner.'

Why not? With any other client it would mean nothing. I agreed to go to the shop and we would go on from there at seven.

Matthew was working late and the children had swimming club and chips after with a friend. It was all too easy. I took time dressing, putting on my new black trouser-suit and a bright top underneath. Why did I bother to put on my best underwear? How sure was I?

Jed had bothered. The battered chinos were replaced by a smart pair of dark cords and a bright shirt. The thick mass of hair looked as if it had been washed and he smelt of expensive aftershave. He was waiting at the door of the shop when I arrived and produced a bunch of gerberas.

'You liked these in the coffee shop,'

'But it's not a date,' I whispered.

He guided me carefully to a small bistro at the end of the road. A thin wire hummed between us. I was afraid to talk. He had reserved a table and we sat opposite each other. My briefcase containing his artwork seemed a redundant prop in the play we were acting out. We both knew that it would happen. We ate very little – a few mouthfuls of pasta and some red wine. Then in a husky voice he said, 'Come home, will you... please?'

And in that second and the perfectly delicious moments that followed, I felt no guilt. I buried the querulous voice of my maiden aunt that had sat on my shoulder prodding my conscience, with the shreds of a tatty tartan rug.

REFLECTIONS OF THE SEA

As I turn the corner from the little lighthouse, past re-whitened, salt-rusting barriers at Porthcawl, and the sea is flung in front of me, thundering grey, topped with briny ice-cream swirls that smack the senses, I remember perfect days in my childhood: the picnics on the beach, the highlight of the summer, when the sun always shone.

My Mum would spend weeks planning the feast, watching the weather, conferring with friends. It had to be fish cakes, not ordinary fish cakes, certainly not shop, but made from small, sweet haddock, eyes bright, bought at daybreak from Swansea Market by Dad, and rushed home as quickly as the old Humber would take him. I knew when I came down for breakfast and saw the giant poacher that it was our special day. Mum would lift off the lid and hold me up to see the plump fish bubbling in a watery nest of carrots, onions, crescents of fresh lemons and chopped celery with their tops tied in a ponytail with masses of fresh parsley, thyme, and bay leaves from the garden. After a few minutes, she would leave the fish to cool, anxiously checking her watch and assembling the rest of the picnic. Then she would take the fish off the bone leaving it in flakes, and mince vegetables, mixed with a bowl of Dad's King Edwards mashed with a good few knobs of local, Welsh, butter, milk, a hint of freshly grated nutmeg, salt and black pepper. Then the mixture would be rolled and shaped in her special concoction of breadcrumbs, oats and sesame seeds and fried in vegetable oil and butter. She always made dozens and they went. They were accompanied by potato salad, rich with homemade mayonnaise and chopped spring onions, chock-filled in heavy glass Kilner jars.

To follow, the tradition was a large crusty blackcurrant or raspberry pie running with juice with maybe a handful of early wimberries plucked from stubby bushes in the Beacons, and local cream, steeped with the fragrant seeds of a vanilla pod. She would insist on bringing jelly and blancmange in another Kilner jar. Dad would be cross because the jars were heavy in the baskets, too much to carry with the deck chairs, the blankets, the wind break, the balls, my painted enamel bucket and spade, and the bottles of pop. But my mother would laugh and we'd get there in the end. The deck chairs extended in a long line of laughing friends swapping tastes: dandelion and burdock, American cream soda, and the odd beer or two.

Then I had to wait for the food to go down, to go into the sea. It took forever and I would hop impatiently from leg to leg waiting in my knitted costume for the minutes to pass.

'Don't go far,' they said. Can you imagine saying that to small children now?

They would give me directions: a row of grown-ups and the new baby, near a white rock, and that would suffice.

Then I ran from the soft sand where the grownups were, to freedom, through the coal-edged ripples and the magical squiggles of worm casts, to the damp hard sand on the edge of a rattle of stones where the wind blew fierce in my hair, and onto the water.

And there was that moment when it was all before me – all mine.

Make it last. Make it last.

Precious like the penultimate minute before bed, or the first ice cream of the summer, I slipped my toes into the grey flutters at the edge – oooh. An intake of iciness.

But you have to go on.

And slowly, I walked. Pushed thin thighs through heavy swirling waves, growing larger – slick animals wet with their own power. Then I tried to sit down, buffeted by those friendly monsters, which threw salty water in my mouth.

I jumped and screamed and it didn't matter. No one was cross, especially the beasts, pitching me even further. I pretended to swim. Flung my head from side to side as I'd seen others do. But I never moved. It didn't matter. Nothing mattered: just the delicious animals that wanted to play. I felt I was there for hours.

Then I grew cold. Darkening shadows over the water told me it was time to return to the grown-ups. I shivered as I pulled myself away. Goose bumps sprouted over my arms and legs. The knitted costume slapped heavy against my body.

Time to go back. But where are they? Where have they gone?

I never told them how scared I was when I couldn't see them. And they were always miles away from where they should be. They'd always changed their place. And the rock?

When I returned, Mum produced yet more food. It would be time for the sandwiches. Dad always made the same joke. 'Everybody. We've got cucumber and sand, and salad and sand.' People laughed. Dad was happy. To accompany the sandwiches were hardboiled eggs, wrapped in two layers of greaseproof paper and a layer of tinfoil, ceremonially peeled on site with crisps and a twist of salt in blue paper. Then there would be thick Welsh Cakes, heavy with currants and butter, chunky slices of Bara Brith and dainty lemon curd tarts tasting sticky-sweet and sharp. To wash the lot down Dad produced another bag with flasks of tea. The tea was his department. With milk concealed in a special container underneath the thermos, he poured a brew they said a mouse could trot across.

I sat, cross-legged on blanket, wrapped in a fluffy towel, licking the lemon curd in a tart and listening to the fun. There was no better moment.

Now all of them, Mum, Dad, aunties and uncles, are faded sepia pictures, in silver frames, resting on my mantelpiece.

But when I turn that corner into Porthcawl or we near Rest Bay, or I eat a hardboiled egg with a dip of salt, I hear them, see them, alive, enjoying, tasting, laughing.

MOTHER OF A SON

Well, that's the couscous made. I hope it's not too exotic for them. I wonder whether that's the kind of food they like? Looks like birdseed to me.

I look across the kitchen table. It's done now – the Friday night meal. They'll be here any second. I've gone to bed with Jamie Oliver and got up with Evelyn Rose. I'm sure Morris would have preferred it the other way.

I made two meals in the end, one for them and one for us. I had to begin the preparations yesterday, there was so much to do. They've got egg and onion to start. I wanted to make my chopped liver. Morris says that my chopped liver is the best in the world. It's because I render the fat from the chicken in a slow pan with a large onion and, when it is cooled, I add the crispy bits, the griebenes in the mincer, to the mixture. Bad for you? Cholesterol? Who cares. My mother and her family always ate it and they never worried about cholesterol. But if it has to be egg and onion, that's still delicious. My secret is that I boil the eggs and then I mix them with some fried onions and some raw chopped spring onion – it adds a lovely colour and freshness to the dish.

Naturally, the next course was going to be chicken soup. Who's ever heard of a Jewish family that won't enjoy chicken soup? I still manage to get an old boiling hen if I can. It goes in the large pot from my mother, with an onion, left whole. The brown parchment skins help to make the soup more golden. Then I add cleaned carrots, celery, with a bit of the green and the giblets. It's best if it's made the day before so that the fat cools over night and can be skimmed off. But of course Ben says that they won't take it, so I've got to make the chicken soup for Morris and a vegetable soup for them. I've got some wonderful recipes. Maybe I'll make mushroom and barley and watch the weight roll on their hips.

Ben came in last week just as I had the order delivered from the butchers.

'Mum', he said. He looked tired and thin. I don't think he gets the rest with her that he used to when he lived at home. I know he has to iron his own shirts – the very idea! 'Mum', he said, 'I know that you are going to a lot of trouble and Miriam and I appreciate it, but do you think that you could make something fishy for Miriam and her parents? You see they are trying to eat more healthily. They don't eat meat at all and it wouldn't be a bad idea if you and Dad...'

A chutzpah! He's telling me how I should feed his girlfriend and her parents! I looked at the boy. You know I'd do anything for my son. Girls are one thing – but a son. My son, a premature baby, raised at the beginning of the seventies when there was all that palaver introducing decimal currency into the UK. Aunty Freda said I would never cope. As if I didn't have enough to do trying to get over the birth and the stitches and run the shop. But I managed. After Dad went, who else could stand there, day after day? It was hard. I'd have to get a bus from Stoke Newington to the East End every morning and then serve, running in between to the baby out the back. Then there would be the orders to do and the buying to arrange. But I managed.

People would come from far and wide just to sniff my pickled herrings. We served them traditionally, out of dark wooden barrels, wrapping them in greaseproof paper parcels. They would lie silky-slimy like plump grey ribbons, mixed with cloves of garlic and frills of dill. The barrels would be arranged next to oak boxes stacked high with smokies, golden-brown smoked fish with toasted skins fresh from Highland smokehouses, layered in their beds in copper togetherness in a perfect pattern. And then there would be the cucumbers, salty Polish in heavy brine. How that liquid would sting the skin if you had a little cut. I could never get on with rubber gloves – on, off, on, off. Then more mellow sweet and sour with a bumpy skin made from small ridge cucumbers – lovely sliced with a cold fish supper. You'd cut plaice across the bone, dip the sections in egg and matzo meal and fry them crispy. Then serve cold with potatoes peeled after boiling, those brown papery skins burning your fingers. The potatoes would be sliced thick, with a rich mayonnaise yellow with eggs, decorated with slivers of the cucumber cut lengthways. And the new green I'd make myself. You'd have to be careful with those bright green chunks of cucumber that they didn't go off. It was only a mild pickle so you still had all the crunch mixed with a hint of sharp. I'd put in a bit of garlic and chilli into those. They think they're so fancy these days with their chilli. I've been doing it for years.

But I loved the breads best. We sold all the kosher breads. If they weren't observed in the baking, then you couldn't make the blessings. We got a dark sourdough bread in from Glasgow. It was so large, like the shoulder of the carthorses that delivered the milk to my mother. We sold a half at a time. There was black bread, very dark. I'd make up a sandwich for Uncle Sim if he came in with black bread and chopped herring and plenty of saltless butter. That was his favourite. I liked the rye studded with caraway seeds, very tasty with cream cheese, or a good bagel, shiny-topped, layered with smoked salmon and more cream cheese. On Friday there used to be such a rush for challot – wonderful traditional plaited breads, each as large as a feather bolster from Freda's big bed and as fluffy. I can remember when we were children and my mother had to make the money go further and we were all starving before Shabbat and she would give us a slice of challah spread with chicken fat – shmaltz – and plenty of salt. It would keep our bellies full and Dad had enough problems to do that with nine children.

Well that's in the past now. They were good times. People were close in those days and they wouldn't dream of refusing a good chicken dinner. I could be offended. My roast chicken isn't good enough. But still, what can you do? He loves this girl and the family seem to have a good name. The father's an accountant. We'll see how good he is with money when they organise the wedding. I hope he's not mean. After all you don't have a wedding every day. I know. Morris and the three girls have told me not to interfere. It's easy for them. They're not the mother. The mother of a son.

When he came round to tell me about their fancy eating habits, he sat opposite me at the blue Formica table in the kitchen, stirring a glass of lemon tea and eating a kichel. I put out a whole plate – lovely biscuits fragrant with lemon rind and vanilla and filled with currants and sultanas. They were always his favourite. I still make them in case he calls round. It's not as often since he's with Miriam. 'I'll only take one,' he says. 'In training' he calls it. I got up to reboil the kettle. I wanted to touch his hair, ruffle its silkiness like I used to do when he was small. I touch his face. He pulls back a little. 'Don't Mum,' he says. 'Don't mess me around'. Impatient like his father. Of course she can touch him. When they walk in the house they are always hand in hand. Did she have to get up every night, the measles, the mumps, that nasty bout of croup when he couldn't catch his breath and had a kind of fit? And how about the bullying when that lad at the end of the road beat him up? It was me who went to see his mother. I remember it was already Shabbat and Ben hadn't arrived back from school. I knew there was something wrong and when he came home blood everywhere and his clothes torn, I was down the road, Shabbat or not. Mrs Thompson was very sorry, so she said. All I know is, he didn't get bullied any more. Is that Miriam going to do that sort of thing for him?

Well, back to this dinner. They won't eat my roast chicken. Not healthy enough. I'm still going to

183

make it for my Morris. He will eat and enjoy it. I'll make them a piece of salmon. I can cook it early in the poacher with carrots, onions and a few slices of lemon and leave it to cool. It will look good cold decorated with slices of cucumber and stuffed olives. When I first heard they were coming and why, I was excited. It's not every day your son decides to get married. Although I wasn't too happy with the current arrangement. You certainly didn't do that sort of thing when I was young. Share a house before the big day. I try to like the girl. I suppose in her own way she's quite pretty – a little plump perhaps. She's most probably on the pill. She seems to wear those tracksuits at the weekend. I know she has a tough job in the city and has to wear a suit every day but that's no reason to let herself go at weekends. I told Ben. I said 'Give her a couple of years and a few children and she'll be huge!' Ben was very angry and didn't come round for a long time after. I'm sure there are plenty of girls who would want my Ben. He's a prince. She's lucky to get him, and her parents. He's always around their house. He says that Doreen, Miriam's mother, is very welcoming and treats him like a son. Well, so she should. He says that they eat a more healthy diet – Mediterranean, he calls it. Seems to me they live on lockshen – they call it pasta. We've been eating it for years in the soup.

I'm still going to make cholent. Friday night wouldn't be Friday night without that wonderful comforting casserole with carrots and prunes and butter beans. It's lovely fresh and it stays in the oven till tomorrow on a slow heat and is just as good. Morris says it gives him indigestion, but how can something as good as that upset him? More likely to be the stress of this engagement. I'll serve the cholent as I always do with potatoes roasted with the shmaltz from the chicken, and a nice cucumber salad sweet and sour. I've done them that couscous I saw in the new Jamie Oliver book that one of the girls brought. I'll show them that I can be fashionable.

The last time I saw Doreen, Miriam's mother, was at a function. She was wearing a black dress, a bit skimpy if you ask me, with pin-thin heels and a hat like a dead bird on the top, well, a lot of feathers, anyway. She's always preening. Says she likes to take care of herself. Who has the time to watch their figure, do their make-up and the nails? Have you seen the length of them?

They said – don't interfere. Leave it alone. So I will, but when she comes to my house, I'm in charge of the kitchen. I'll nobble her perfect figure over the dessert. She'll have to eat some to be polite. I'll make a lockshen pudding with double the marg'. Make her fat. Make her sick? Should I worry? She's given me enough worry. She's given me anxieties with her daughter. Ben was happy before he met her. He would sit in the kitchen with me drinking tea. He'd take me to cards and come back at the end. So attentive, so perfect. Then he was happy to eat a chicken dinner like everyone else. Now he's gone fussy and miserable and doesn't want his mother. She's poisoned him – made her daughter say things so that he hates me. It's that Doreen and her daughter's fault. I'll give them dessert – their just deserts.

I get out the lockshen and I boil it up. I beat margarine with sugar, grated lemon rind and juice and add them with grated apple. I'm angry. I want to add bags of sharp pins, bitter aloes, but I put in extra margarine. Give her a bit of fat; worry about a few pounds. To go with the pudding, I make a chocolate mousse, with egg yolks and bitter chocolate and brandy, as rich as a Yomtov goose. Now we'll show her who's in charge – who's the cook round here.

I went to bed angry last night. I dreamt of my son with that girl – of Jamie Oliver, and Evelyn Rose with my Morris.

They'll be here in a minute. Check the table. Everything ready.

SHADOW OF A
DRAGONFLY

'Well, that must be everything cleared now. Come on. I'll be glad to get out and have a coffee.'

'In a minute. I've just got to... '

'You're not going all sentimental on us are you, Mona? I've been through everything. Anything important was whisked off by her daughter straight after the funeral. There's just that weird old basket, full of mouldering clothes – moth-holes and beads dropping off. Looks like even the dealers didn't want it. Don't blame them. The smell was awful. And dozens of empty flower baskets. Spooky really. Faded ribbons and messages, covered in dust... disgusting. Five black bags, for goodness sake – just for those! And those hundreds of scraps of letters –' Liz shuddered and wiped dusty hands over her official overall. 'Come on, love, there's nothing here anymore. Let's go.'

'I can't... not for a minute... I'll meet you later. We'll have a sandwich together? Where are the things?'

'Oh, I've bunged them by the back entrance ready for the bin men. You're not going to pull them all out now and make a mess.'

'No mess. I promise.'

Liz slammed the door and Violet's last domain answered with a dusty echo: thin walls vibrating like a banjo's belly. I had to stay. Had to make my final journey through Violet's life. Was it only two months ago the Warden had rung me? It had been late – eleven thirty – and her voice was shrill.

'Violet's becoming impossible – I've told her she must lock her front door. She knows it's dangerous but she will leave it open, and now she's refusing to let the cleaners in and the other residents are complaining of the smell. You're the only one she'll listen to. Sort it, Mona, please, or I'll have to report to Mr Stafford.'

'No, no. I'll go tomorrow. I promise.'

Early the next day, I walked up the staircase to number 23. Net curtains twitched with relish at Violet's imminent castigation. A fetid mix of rotten fruit, general neglect and parma violets choked my throat. I stopped for a second. Took a mint out of my bag to try to offset the stench. Then, with a deep breath, I walked in. 'Violet love... it's Mona.'

Give Me Back My Broken Dolly crackled on the phonograph. The curtains were pulled tight and the few lampshades, some waxy parchment, others faded silk with most of their beads lost in the passage of time, cast pools of light into corners stacked with papers and empty flower baskets. I tried to ignore them. Violet's chair was placed throne-like in the corner of the room. She sat there – chiaroscuro, only her face visible in the half light – a tiny shrivel of a person, the ancient carpet below her feet swamped by a mass of boxes of photographs and old sheet music. She looked at me through black bead eyes. 'The old bag has sent you to give me a telling off. Hasn't she? Shut your door! You must let the cleaners in. Blah Blah blah!'

'I thought I'd come to visit you, Violet. Shall I make us a cup of tea?'

A twisted claw-hand raised in acknowledgement. She nodded: her skin etched with nearly a century's lines.

'Alright, darling... ' Her voice changed. 'You won't move anything out there, will you?'

'No. No.'

Then her face wreathed with smiles. 'You got cream cakes in that box?'

I picked my way through the piles of papers into the small kitchenette. The odour intensified. In the middle of the kitchen table fruit lay mouldering in its ancient glass bowl: above it, a small cloud of flies. The bowl squatted on a tablecloth of newspaper next to an open tin of condensed milk, a half eaten white sliced loaf, and a knife with a chipped ivory handle. A cracked plastic bin spewed foil food containers, some half-undone, and neatly labelled.

'Don't eat that much,' she chirped from the other room, anticipating my questions. 'Don't trust those dinners – all those metal packets – they say aluminium does your brains in – gives you Alzheimer's – and I'm

OK in the box. Anyway, they've got germs – they're trying to knock me off, 'cos I'm trouble.'

'No, Violet, love – they're balanced meals specially prepared for you.'

'Well, I don't trust 'em and I'm not eating 'em, so there! How's that tea going?'

I looked about the kitchenette, trying to ignore the odour from sink and bins.

'Where are your cups, Violet?'

'In the bloody sink waiting for you to wash 'em. Did I see a cream cake box?'

I rolled up my sleeves, emptied the sink, found a packet of unopened black bags and threw a pile of the mouldering packets into one, then washed all the dishes.

'Gosh, Mona... didn't know you were the new cleaner. I'd 'ave let you in,' cackled Violet.

I returned with two cracked cups of tea on a metal tray, no saucers, the box of cream cakes and two plates, now clean.

'Shall I open the curtains so you can see better to choose which cakes you want?'

'No. No. It's safer like this.'

I pulled up a small piano stool that must have been upholstered, originally in an ecru silk. Now it was dun – the colour of dirt. Then I moved one of the boxes, placed the tray over the open top and slid the whole bounty over to Violet.

She licked her lips in anticipation, extended bone-hands like pincers over the box. 'Which one are you having?' she said, eyeing the doughnut, the éclair, and strawberry tart.

'I don't mind... choose two.'

'I shall have the éclair and the strawberry tart. They look a little like the patisseries we had in France when I was young.'

'I didn't know you lived in France?'

'That was another world.'

'Do you have family there?'

'Maybe. But that's my secret.'

The old lady ate with relish, sucking on fingers for vestiges of icing, cream, then wetting her fingers and pushing them onto the last few crumbs in the box.

'When did you last have a meal, Violet?'

'I don't know... the loaves go mouldy so quickly. You can buy me one if you like.'

An idea flashed through my mind. I would be breaking regulations. But what the hell. I liked the old girl and she was starving.

'Violet. What's your favourite food?'

Her fingers were still stubbing in the end of the box and the head with its wisps of silver remained lowered. 'Fish and chips, darling, nice and greasy out of the newspaper... none of those bloody tins... with plenty of malt vinegar and salt.' She raised her face, licked her lips and her eyes dreamed of a far-off taste.

'Well, Violet, supposing I brought my tea here tonight and I bought fish and chips for you. Do you think we could talk a little more... try to sort things out?'

The bird eyes flashed with excitement. 'What, you'll come here with real fish and chips... and you'll get me a white sliced as well? OK then.'

'And you promise we'll talk?'

'Mmm...' The head had returned to the box.

I walked into the kitchen, rinsed the plates and cups, then moved to the door. 'I'll be here at six, Violet.'

'Don't worry, the door will be open,' she cackled. 'Don't forget to bring the white loaf. I like the thick slices...'

I returned to the council office and pulled out Violet's file. She was indeed French. Violette de l'Eau. Born in Paris, 1910... mother Bijou de l'Eau. Father unknown. Likes now to be called Violet... final employment... theatrical landlady, Brighton... previously appeared on stage in Music Hall.

The evening came quickly. Violet had made some effort. The old white loaf and the fruit with its cloud of flies had gone, and a clean sheet of newspaper lay on the kitchen table.

'Thought I'd clear up a bit in your honour.' She leaned back on a polished ebony cane with a silver-looking top, eyeing the grease-stained packets in my hand.

'You've done really well,' I said, trying not to sound patronising. 'While I'm putting these on plates, why don't I just get rid of a few of these foil containers. Make a bit more room in here. You could pop back to your chair and I'll bring in our supper when the kettle's boiled. Tea with it?'

Violet nodded. She looked tired and leaned over the cane. I slipped my hand into the crook of her arm, felt bones clad in wrappings of worn silk and woollies, and led her gently to her chair. 'Violet, love. I'll go and get our supper.' I returned to the kitchen, found plates and piled up the fish and chips.

'Mmm... smells luscious.' Violet smacked her lips. But she ate very slowly, chewing with a dry mouth and swallowing with difficulty.

'That's a lovely cane you use, Violet,' I said.

'That's from when I trod the boards... a long time ago now.'

'Really? Oh, Violet, do tell me about it.'

'Don't mind. If you want to know?'

I nodded. 'Of course I do.'

'I came over from France in 1928, and with me training it was easy to get into Music Hall – there were loads in them days. Palaces they were, all decorated with gold and cherubs and glittering chandeliers. Plush crimson and wine-coloured curtains... front stage... with massive gold tassels and, sometimes, in the older places, we'd 'ave the old gas foot lights on the apron... 'ave to watch the full skirts... many of them crinolines... with all the wires. I used to sing a bit... had a nice figure, showed a bit of ankle and wore me old Paris costumes with the fish-net stockings.' She lifted a chip and conducted an imaginary orchestra. Then bent over slightly as if taking a bow. 'I always did a few saucy songs in me repertoire to get 'em going... they said I was the new Marie Lloyd. She died in 1922 and had a huge funeral with 50,000 people, you know. It was a good life... Mind you, if you'd seen them dressing rooms. Like bloody rat tunnels... boiling hot or freezing cold. Once I had to share with Francine and her Ferrets and the ferrets got out. Ooh, there was a palaver... those little stinkers running around... took four of us ages to catch 'em.' Her eyes crinkled and the tiny shoulders hunched up, in a laugh. 'But my best moment was when I appeared on the same bill with Vesta Tilley at Wilton's – the finest Music Hall in the country. She was a performer who impersonated men! It was a good show... the audience loved it.... we were sold out for weeks. Then one night I had a bad fall... broke me hip getting to the dressing room in a rush, and couldn't kick me leg up anymore, so I decided to pack in the theatre – there's nothing worse than an act when it's dying... I put my bit of money into a little boarding house at the seaside in Hove. Oh I still knew all the troupers. They'd come to stay. They'd be working on the end of one of the piers, summer season or whatever and we had some fun. Plenty of laughs in them days. They all loved me you know.'

'I'm sure they did, you must have been very popular, and, was there someone special?'

'What you mean, a man – a lover? You want to know if I had a man in my life? Yes, darling, loads and loads... But special?'

'Was there?'

'No one. Not special. Of course there was Emma's Dad but he didn't last long... he blamed me, of course... said I was never satisfied... said he couldn't be a mother as well as a partner. Silly sod! But in a way he was right. I never found the love in me to... Well, that was the fault of bloody Paris. Wasn't it?'

I looked at her, waiting for the next few words hoping at last for her secrets. But it was as if a trapdoor in her memory had snapped shut.

'Can't talk anymore.' She shut her eyes and said weakly, 'Thanks for supper, love. It was smashing... just like the old days.'

I carried out the detritus of our meal – it looked as if Violet had hardly started – washed up quickly and, as I was going, touched the old lady's arm.

'I won't be able to come for a couple of weeks. It's my spring leave. But I'll tell Liz to call. You like Liz, don't you?' I knew the old lady wouldn't be happy. Guilt twisted my gut. 'I'll shut the door OK?' Though I knew that as soon as Violet had gathered up a bit of strength, the door would be wide open again.

As soon as I returned from holiday I could tell from Liz's face that something had happened.

'Mona love. I did try... honestly. I went in a few times with a sliced white loaf and a tin of condensed, as you asked, then a couple of days ago, we were notified by the Warden. They took her into geriatric yesterday.'

'Thanks for going. I knew she was poorly... nobody's fault.'

She was at the far end of a busy ward. I spoke to the sister. 'She's stable at last – she's had quite a few units and she's got a bit more colour now. We've got her out of bed this morning... that wasn't easy.'

She sat in the corner – a tiny thing trapped on a mass of pillows in a large hospital chair.

'Hello Violet... I was so sorry to...'

'Bugger off... I thought you were my friend. Look what they've done to me!' She raised a wasted arm swathed in bandages. It was still attached to a drip and at the point of attachment was a vast purple bruise. It was as if the bone itself was cloaked in purple skin.

'I'm sorry, love. I did tell you I had to take time off.'

195

Violet reached down next to her seat. She wasn't listening.

'Some silly little girl in a white coat came round and said I had to weave something. Making bloody baskets with these fingers. I told her I couldn't manage. Anyway I got her to make most of it. You might as well 'ave it. I can't hold the bloody thing properly. Anyway I only like baskets with flowers in 'em... that last bloody cleaner tried to get rid... get rid of me baskets! They 'ad me flowers when I was the star... and... and all me lovely messages... got rid of 'er all right. She won't be back.'

With great effort, she pulled out a hardboard tray with holes punched into it. A cane edge was woven around it.

'Thank you, Violet. I appreciate that.' She looked utterly exhausted. 'I'll leave now. But I'll come again in a couple of days.'

I was at home, just getting ready to visit Violet, when the phone rang. It was Mr Stafford from our office. 'It's Violet... she's insisting on seeing you immediately. I understand you have some kind of relationship...?'

'Yes, yes... I'll come.'

The old lady was propped up on an arrangement of pillows. Where her legs and torso rested there seemed little difference in the board-flatness of the covers. They had raised the sides of the bed to make a metal cot. It looked like a chrome cage. Her face was white with two pins of fever pink in her cheeks.

'I want to talk about France. I want you to understand why... why it wasn't my fault.'

I pulled up a stool from under the bed and took one of the tiny hands.

'My mother was famous. First an actress, then an artist's model. She modelled for Rene Lalique and then Georges Barbier... her face and her body were famous all over France. I arrived as a nuisance. She was angry... said I ruined her body. She told me she didn't know who my father was... not important to her. She said I had many fathers. Mornings I would smell cigarettes and hot coffee in the kitchen... a rustle of the red silk sheets and another man would walk into the kitchen naked except for trousers or a towel. I had to call these men *Mon Oncle*, and curtsy... that's how I thought life was. After I was born, she put me into an open drawer... then... as I started to toddle, she stuck me in a bloody props basket... I can remember it now. I hated the damn thing... scratchy wicker... high sides.' An emaciated hand rubbed the itch of old prickles. 'I've hated being locked in ever since. Open doors... that's what you need... open doors... As soon as I was old enough she put me with the variety acts – the dogs – the clowns... had to earn my keep. She was modelling... she'd become the face of Art Nouveau. So many times I watched as she contorted her body... leaning into a pose. Then one day Monsieur Lalique decided that she would look even more beautiful as a dragonfly. It was difficult... she had to be tied to a structure, like a crucifix, and then, when her arms and legs were bound tightly into position, huge gossamer wings painted silver and lilac were attached to her back. She became a star. "Female form and nature," that's what they called her... Famous all over France... She only drank champagne and sat like a queen surrounded by flowers with ribbons and messages. Now and then she would remember me, sometimes swearing at me as she rubbed the stigmata of bonding after hours of modelling. But I knew her best as a rustle of silk or a whiff of perfume. Then, one day, just before my eighteenth birthday, Monsieur Lalique asked my mother if I could pose for him. After he left she turned to me and screamed crazy words... I can still see her taffeta peignoir – marabou trimmed – in me mind... crackling like silver ice. She growled at me. Her mouth spat curses.

'You must have slept with him. Why else would he want you? You're not the beautiful one. I am!' The old lady was pulling herself up in the bed. I tried to help her back into the pillows.

'That's why I ran away. I never slept with him. Or anyone. I just wanted my mother to love me... to know that I loved her. But she didn't want to hear it. She never wanted...

'I took a boat to England and started in the Music Hall and I've 'ad an all right life but I always wanted her to... that's why it never worked with... Look, love. All the photos and messages. If you want any just take 'em, and the bloody props basket if you want it.'

Was it only a few days ago? The flat reeks of Jeyes Fluid. Violet's belongings are a pile of black bags in a corridor waiting for the bin men. I look through thousands of letters. Each says *with love*, or *fond affection* and those words have been underlined in scratchy ink strokes. At the bottom of the one bag I find a small sepia postcard of The Dragonfly – Le Bijou de l'Eau – twisted into an extraordinary pose, and one of Violet's foil wrapped dinners stuck to the face.

I AM A TIGER

As she walks into the club I know my life will never be the same.

'Fancy an old un then, Dai?' says Rhys, nudging me. I shove him away. But there's a stir of something, like on a Saturday night when Megan's asked me to dance, or one of the other girls from the college. She swings over to the bar on clattering stilettos – black, six inch with bows on the back and an air of knowing what she is about. I'd say she's maybe fortyish but well kept, plump and sleek like one of those seals that lazed on the pointy rocks round the waters of the Lleyn Estuary when we visited last summer.

'Coming then?'

'No... no... I'll catch you up later.'

There's belly punching and some shoulder bashing and a lot of laughter and they're gone. Down the High Street to toss a coin in their minds and chase thoughts of a curry so hot it would fire their throats, or a fishy battered feast dipped in salt and liquid with malt vinegar.

Why do I stay? I can hear their mirth jabbing in the wind, the echoes of their feet chasing a rattling can down the steep valley road excavated out of grey rocks spiked with gorse. Lined with barbed wire fences hastily erected last year when skins of sheep lay empty, their bodies rustled for meat.

The music plays an old beat and now we are on our own – apart from Gus the D.J. who looks as if he wants to pack up, and Julie behind the bar who put on her slippers hours ago and keeps yawning and looking at her watch.

'Hiyah,' she says.

'Fancy a drink?'

'Yeh. OK. Something long with ice.' She's got a husky voice that's a cocktail of smoke and sex.

'Bacardi and coke, something like that?'

'Sounds lovely.'

She's moving next to me and sliding onto one of those stools designed for men. She finds it difficult to climb up and make herself comfortable. Finally she crosses her legs under her slippery skirt and the material edges up high over her knees.

'I've seen you around. David, isn't it?'

'Yes.'

She looks directly at me – no shyness, with her eyes dark and liquid like my Mam's spaniel and just as soft and friendly. I glance down quickly. It's as if she can read my thoughts. She takes a slow deliberate sip of her drink, lowers her gaze and looks straight at me again.

'Why didn't you go with the others?'

200

'Bit of a gippy stomach – not hungry.' *Why do I lie? She can see through my daft excuses.*

She traces a figure eight with a manicured finger over the ice-bloom of the glass. Then takes that finger chilled and damp and rubs the skin next to my watch.

'What time is it then?'

I'm fired with an electric charge.

'Half past... half past one.'

'Christ, I've got to go,' she says.

'Let me see you home?'

I offer some coins to Julie who yawns gratefully, puts her slippers into a Peacock's bag and pulls her coat off the peg.

We go out together arm in arm, bodies unfamiliar but strangely comfortable. Out of the light and the smoke and the smell of beer. Into the rain and the hollows of darkness and the shivery wind. It's beginning to drizzle – the spring day that had started with so much promise of blue in the sky has changed its mind and dropped into pit-black and cold. She trembles as the wind lances through her shoulders. *Why didn't I have a big coat to put about her like they do in the films?* I'm dressed just in my shirt and I can feel her body, just little straps to her dress and a thin cardigan taut about her.

I put my arm around her tight.

'Best get you home quick... it's turned nasty now.'

We walk almost in an embrace and it's so good. She's about five foot two and there's me over six feet but she kind of fits into the crook of my arm and I'm enjoying the feeling. And she tells me her name – Chantelle – and I want more. Then she pulls away and begins to clatter down the steep of the road laughing with her voice bouncing in the gutters, deep and throaty. I chase with my big damn size twelves echoing loud on the tarmac to the bottom of Hanbury Road.

It's a small street the same as ours, stiff terraced houses with their stone faces shut to the wind. Each painted a bright colour looking like my gran and her friends sat at the Senior Citizens Club when they've fished out the multicoloured hand-knits to look cheerful.

'It's here,' she says.

And from a small fuchsia bag covered with sparkly bits she pulls out a bunch of keys, clicks one in the lock and dusts a kiss on my cheek.

'Come for your tea on Wednesday,' she whispers huskily. 'I'll make you something, OK? Maybe Chinese if your stomach's better? Bout seven?'

She brushes my cheek with her mouth and is gone, through the white doorway with the lilac front door. It slams shut and I try to see her through a deep window with curtains hanging in lacy swags over a pair of china dogs and pink plastic roses in a vase.

I walk back to ours touching my face. I'm dazed. Her perfume floats round my arms, stronger in the damp. Finally I'm back. I know it's our place because there are three black bags of rubbish sprawled next to the path like drunks. I slide the key into the lock and open the door gently. I don't want to talk – just hold onto the moment. As I stand inside the doorway, I pick off my shoes at the bottom of the stairs.

But suddenly, downstairs is full of light and noise and the horn they use at the rugby blasting. The boys are laughing and pushing me and joking. They look like three puppies waiting for a treat, tongues lolling and tails wagging.

'Surprise! What was she like then? Come on. Did she? Did you? Tell lad, tell.'

'Don't be so daft, mun. I walked her home that's all.'

'That's all. That's all. But didn't you?'

'No… no I didn't.' I can feel the red rushing up to my face. So I take my shoes tight in my one hand and I push past Ben who has moved to the bottom of the stairs and thinks he's got me cut off. But he hasn't. Like a gladiator I'm up and into my room and pressed against the bedroom door, heart throbbing in my chest. The footsteps follow and they are giggling and pounding my door. But they get tired and I'm left to remember her and that she's cooking me tea on Wednesday, and…

Next morning, I'm in college – I'm doing City and Guilds Catering at Ystrad. I want to be one of those flashy chefs with my own programme and my name embossed on the side of frying pans and videos. I walk into the bakery – a large noisy place full of scrubbed silvered pans as if the giants have taken over. There's a smell of buttery, flaky pastry – yesterday's vanilla slices, and coconut. We're doing the choux variety today – dodgy if you don't know what you're doing. It's an emulsion and you've got to start by beating the flour with the hot fat and water mixture until it's a large shiny ball. And then when it's cooled off, just slip drops of the egg into the mix, sneaky like, so it just gets silkier and silkier… the secret's in the beating. It takes masses of strength but I'm up to it. Some of the puny lads have to use a mixer and there's nothing wrong in that, but it's a bit of a boast if you can get the rise in the pastry without. The morning goes well apart from Megan making odd faces at me behind Mr

Hopkins' back. She was a sort of girl-friend, well, we used to go out sometimes. Not much. She wants to make it into something more and I'm not ready for the serious stuff yet. But she keeps trying and now I pretend I haven't noticed. I'll have to tell her sometime. But I don't know how to do it without hurting her.

I'm creating swans and choux fingers and filling them with synthetic cream. Synthetic cream is disgusting science fiction stuff. It's made from a white fat which is whipped up with vanilla essence and icing sugar and as it whisks it just keeps growing like a ghostly white monster and you can get gallons from a half kilo of fat.

This afternoon we have to make the pastries again, this time with real whipped cream and crème patissière – that's confectioner's custard. Gorgeous. I might buy a few of those and drop them down the road to Chantelle to tell her how much I'm looking forward to Wednesday. That's if I can do it without the boys watching. Otherwise there'll be so many jokes about whipped cream and an older woman, I don't think I could bear it.

I've bought four pastries and found a plastic Tesco's bag in a cupboard, and I decide to drop them off before I go back home. I walk quickly through the ice air, sharp after the heat of the kitchens, with my open mouth a dragon spewing frozen smoke. As I walk I try to recall the gravelly voice and the tightness of silk on flesh. I'm at the lilac front door knocking and I can feel my heart thudding. But the house sounds hollow and through the letterbox I can see that it's dark inside.

Stupid lad, she might have gone out for the evening. You don't know where she works: you don't know what she does...

204

even if she's married? You know nothing about her. All you know is her name, Chantelle Williams – goddess...

I write a note, pop it in the bag, tie a knot in the top of the bag, and hang the parcel from the straggles of last year's hanging basket hoping no one will steal it. Then I go back to the lads and the mess and the cans. It's my turn to cook and I search in the back of the fridge and meet green and blue spotted growths that must have been a frozen pizza. I won't clean it away tonight - can't face it. So I'm doing a trick taught to me by a student from last year. Four pot noodles in a row and four coffees with the milk added in the same row, plus a few rolls from college. Boil up a very large kettle of water, then, if you're lucky, you can pour the water in a steady stream filling all the pots and the mugs at once. Good job the bosses at the college can't see.

'Oh it's the pot noodle trick is it? Can't concentrate on the cooking then? Your mind on other things? What's Megan going to say then?'

They tease, knowing that I usually make an effort when it's my turn. Well, I use them as guinea pigs. Eventually they get sick of mocking and become absorbed in an article in the paper. It's a light-hearted read that tells you about the Chinese New Year and what kind of animal you are in the Chinese Zodiac. One of the lads was born a year before me and he's a rabbit which is 'a delicate animal, kind and sweet'. That makes us all laugh. Rhodri is a year younger than me and has just started in college. He loves it when he reads that he's an ox, 'hard working and persistent'.

'I'll have to tell my mother that it says in the paper I'm hard working... perhaps she'll believe at last,' he chuckles. 'Go on then, read yours.'

As they've been reading and jawing, I've cast my eye over Rhodri's shoulder. It says 'Tiger... born leader is the key word for tigers... Noble and fearless... Tigers are respected for their courage even by those working against them.'

I am a tiger. I know now that Wednesday is meant to be. These things happen. Fate has designed our destinies.

Tuesday limps slowly. Luckily most of it is practical so I can muddle through with my mind down the hill at the house with the lilac front door. Lunchtime I sit with Megan and a few of the girls whose voices rise and bubble like the neon-bright bottles of pop they drink in the canteen. Now and then I catch their words.

'What you going to wear then?' 'How many are going?' ' Oh purple top black trousers' '... going into Cardiff this Saturday, Dai?'

'Dai... Dai. We need to talk... Dai? Megan prods me with a slim finger tipped with a chip of blue nail polish.

'OK... sometime... I'll see... not today though.'

My mind is on tomorrow, and tea at Chantelle's.

*   *   *

Last night I dreamt of tigers, vast gleaming cats with honed claws and glistening teeth. My younger brother had a book for his birthday on India and we talked about Indian mythology and the tiger god Vaghadeva as a bringer of fertility and the ceremonial tiger dances that take place along the southern coast of India. And how one day we would go there and discover one of the last remaining wild tigers together.

The day slopes into evening, and I skip the last two lectures to bathe without jeers. On the way home I buy fine green points of daffodils – first of the season.

I'm out of the door, clean shirt, pressed cargos, smelling good. I borrowed a squirt of Rhodri's after-shave and I feel fluttery like a young girl. Down the hill fast, my feet crunching on a crisp frosty pavement and the sky is gritty with stars. In seconds I'm there at her house, ringing, and waiting. Oh my lord, she comes to the door in a dressing-gown – a glorious red satin thing with dragons embroidered. The tiger in me is screaming – yes!

'Sit down love,' she whispers, 'I've made a cracking sweet and sour chicken with a nice bit of rice in the oven. I've put a bottle of wine in the fridge with a few beers. You can serve them in a minute... .Oh there's the bell...

'... Do you know my niece Megan?'

Megan walks in wearing a tight-cropped silver top and a margin of a skirt. She's got glittery bits all over her skin and the highest pair of heels with legs stretching up to...

She looks at me all dressed up, and Chantelle in her dressing gown. Then Chantelle slowly sits on the pink dralon unaware, smiling. I watch Megan. She covers her face, as if in slow motion, with her hands cupping a cry. But her eyes show... Damn... I didn't want it like this!

On the coffee table in front of the couch sit the choux swans on a fancy plate.

FLESH

Chef's been asking for it.
I sharpen the knives and lay them out on the shivering surface. Cold, scalpel-sweet: each with a purpose. The ten-inch slicer with serrated edges, the eight-inch carving knife also serrated, a five-inch boning knife that severs sinews. And my pride and joy – the cleaver, an almost rectangular slice of honed steel, able to split a head in half or work a piece of bone till it is mush. They are sharpened and placed in a row, sleeping, waiting to be used.

I pick up the boning knife. Listen to the white noise of its tension. Slip the edge of the blade against the heel of my thumb. Kiss the palm of my hand and then draw its sharpness down gently against my stubbled cheek so that skin, blood and bone are so exquisitely near that they could all be mine in a whisper.

But is that the way? Do I want to see an ending, so perfect, so futile? I am sure there is more. I dream when I'm alone, and think of Chef, the pathetic walls of my room, oozing damp, crawling with lice. Outside my window, trains chatter with migraine monotony. I lie on a grey mattress with a roll up and a cheap bottle. The world around me squeezed by the tourniquet of poverty. I look at the knives again in my mind, and say *no*, that is not the answer.

In the late, early hours, at a time of milkmen and postmen, after work, I walk down streets that are dark even when it is light. Where birds have forgotten their songs and I think of him again.

The walls are narrow and daubed with the graffiti of the desperate, chanting voices of mad men. The cries of the ensnared.

Some came here like me, from another rotten place, where they saw us as bad people because we prayed in another way, or our families were reviled because of our colour. We were born in a tradition of hatred.

But I had my chance. 'Go,' they said, 'leave us and try again.' They found money to pay for me to go. I felt proud that my family would use all our savings to buy my freedom. 'I will work hard – look after the family – send money' I said.

For a second my mother smiled, the worry emptied from her face – she looked younger. She pushed a calloused hand through my hair. 'Yes,' she said, 'I know you are a good boy.'

Then she turned her bent back to me. I knew she was crying.

I walked for miles – a barbed wire route – carrying a small bag. It held items for shaving, some bread, a plastic bottle of water, a small blanket and my prayer book. Finally, I found my transport – a cattle truck. There were many of us. We had to sit squashed together. Then, off that truck and into a container. No light, no sound, no air. We couldn't breathe. Some of the girls fainted with the stench. We mustn't complain. Then we seemed to be on a boat. Twisting movements floating light, then shuddering down, dragged onto the rust steel floor. More muffled sounds. A thumping and banging. We could only guess. Cranking and the unlocking of metal bolts and the door was opened. Sweet black air. I am grateful. Dear Lord I am grateful. No time to pray – run in the dark. My new country. Freedom! Safety!

Except they loathe me here. My building is known and they came with flames poured on wet cloths and pushed them through spaces into my room. Now I am scarred.

Where do I go to escape these people? Should I go back – return to the torturers? Stand with the bowed heads, shiver with fear at the whine of a car, or the crunch of footsteps in the night? And, after days of running, avoiding uniforms, know still that bullets lie softly in guns. Until I am no longer a person with an identity, soul, or purpose, but a piece of flesh to be eliminated: and then, an inconvenient carcass to be covered with lime, or left as carrion for the rats and flies.

They will not do this in my new civilised country. Still you see the disgust in their eyes. Cold people. Trained to do their jobs efficiently. To handle us as flesh, as animals, not people like them. After, they return to their families, to suppers out, to embracing wives in warm beds. Their rooms are carpeted and papered and decorated with plants, paintings and books. At night they sleep and do not regret. They are paid cheques and say to their friends that it's a job and that someone has to do it. And the next day they return with their trained dogs that snuffle into our corners.

So I stay in my room dressed in the garment of my fear. When I sleep I have nightmares.

For now I have to content myself with the thought of these knives and what they could do to him. How I wish I didn't work in the stinking belly of this place, scrubbing the scum and rejected lumps of food from other people's plates, and sharpening knives for the chefs. The big one – the one I hate – he calls me 'dog'. He whimpers when he sees me and scrapes the pot scraps on the floor. Then, when I try to pick them up, he kicks me. Once he found my book of prayer sleeping in my coat pocket. He snatched it with his greasy chef hands and threw it in the oven with the roasting flesh.

'Get it, Dog...!' he laughed. 'Get it boy... get it... quick... quick!'

Hot fat spluttered white sparks; coloured flames licked over the sacred pages as it lay on its pyre. My scarred hands still raw from the last agony. I had to... I forced them in to save the words. But the blue silk covers were gone and most of the blessed letters scorched.

Now when I say my prayers, the words are burnt and instead of thinking of Allah I think only of revenge. But I yearn to slip into this society. Be part of the faceless faces that journey without taunts, to return to a safe place – a home with others that care. I pray that one day all my people are together and we are proud again. We will be a nation praying, laughing and singing. We will be allowed to work at what we desire and permitted to succeed. Walk through friendly streets. Sit at pavement cafés and enjoy a coffee in the evening's respite. Play with a football in fields silent from abuse. Watch the dance of the wagtail in the sunlight over river-rippled stones. Rest gently on soft white pillows, have rooms with carpets, and sets of new dishes that match. The women will nurse the babies and the children will study in school and be treated the same as their fellows.

I will have knives of my own and I will cut up flesh and it will be used for celebrations and the flesh will roast and our stomachs will be full and we will have names and be individuals again.

A WELLINGTON BOOT LIFE

'I hated it when he did it, all that pumping away – silly bum in the air. I kept thinking... damn, just get the whole blasted thing over with.'

Paulette leaned over to top up her glass to the brim. Then sank back into the angle of the black leather, caressing the stem, and lifted her flat-heeled shoes onto the glass coffee table. 'I hated the whole stupid thing. I wished I'd never... ' She stopped. She was talking to herself. Letting herself go. It had been just one of those disgusting experiences women tell themselves are about Destiny and Pleasures, but, when it comes to the crunch, there's nothing there at all.

Like buying new shoes. They all raved about that. Paulette could never understand the fuss about straight six inch or kitten heels and chopped off toes and the way that cutesy–pink leather caressed the feet...

Oh... oh you must have paid loads for them... have you felt the leather... so soft. Raptures over a pair of shoes? The girls in the office moaned in ecstasy if they saw a plastic bag from Ian French.

You've got a bag from Ian French... Oh let's see... Oh aren't they gorgeous? Were they expensive? I bet you had to have them though?

Total orgasm over a piece of leather, for goodness sake! You couldn't wear them out in the rain, couldn't do anything with them really. Now trainers, good trainers, supported your ankles: enabled you to walk and run faster.

Paulette had waited a long time for her moment with Don. In school and college it was the other girls who dated – the dolly birds with the short skirts and the pouting lips. She'd tried pouting in a mirror once - on her thirteenth birthday. Spent ages looking at herself after applying a borrowed lipstick. But the red pout resembled the nightmare squirt of jam that landed on her kindergarten face and dress while eating a doughnut that time years before. Gran told her off, said she was a little girl and should want to be more careful with her dress. Paulette reckoned it was daft to make her wear fancy clothes when she was only going round to her Gran's for the day. After all, when Gran wasn't looking, her mother Bernice was quite happy to dress her in the same ankle length, bottle-green dress for days with the badges of every meal glued to her chest. Paulette hated that dress. Her mother had bought it in a fit of guilt while buying the three boys' school uniforms. The only thing in the shop for a girl. The other children in the nursery teased her, said she looked like a cucumber, like a dill pickle in their Dad's takeaway. She pretended to laugh and hid it in the toy cupboard. But her Mum found it again. Mum said that as her Daddy had died just before she was born, they didn't have the money to spend on fripperies and she had too much to do to shop for special outfits just for her. And it was prudent to recycle the boys' clothes. When her mother attempted to dress her in her brothers' trousers, Paulette howled. Between muffled sobs she hiccupped that the boys had left their willies in there, and, she was sure if she wore them, she would grow one too!

And shoes. Wellingtons in winter and sandals for the summer – scuffed brown with a bar strap. Paulette clunked through her childhood in oversized black Wellingtons.

She felt disregarded. As if once her mother had named her child after her late husband, she'd done all that was necessary. Paulette asked her once, 'Why haven't I got a real name like other children? They all laugh at *my* name.' She was sitting at the kitchen table, tongue out, trying to write Pau... le... tte in chubby red wax crayons in a colouring book, over outlines of princes and princesses, next to a roll of toilet paper, a bottle of sherry, two greasy glasses, a miscellaneous pile of letters, old newspapers and a woolly hat.

'You have a proper name,' argued Bernice. 'You are named after your father Paul who was a wonderful man.' Bernice grabbed the roll of toilet paper and began to cry. Paulette never discussed it again. Bernice floated through life assisted by alcohol and Prozac. Paulette had to put herself to bed at four years old.

By the age of eighteen, Paulette carried the stamp of her family. Her body was angular and her stance as if her clothes still contained coat hangers. Her elbows sharp in tailored shirts, her jaw firm. University was a hurdle easily jumped. She applied to those furthest from the wasting atmosphere of booze and tablets. She qualified with the highest marks at the University of Aberdeen, then moved to London to join a firm of City traders.

Her dedication in a man's world was rewarded. Soon she was dealing on the floor, and then head of her department. The men feared her. Everyone knew that Paulette Cliff had balls. So how she succumbed at an office party, as if she was one of the new juniors, no one knew. She was seen with Donald Cox that New Years' Eve drenched in the heady odour of whisky and ginger. It was the first time anyone had seen her drunk. Paulette didn't know herself. As if something had snapped.

She found herself giving Don her key to her apartment, as her own fingers were incapable. She heard his gasp of admiration as they entered. Her flat overlooked the Thames and was decorated with good sculptures, paintings. But Paulette was not in the mood to give a tour.

'The bedroom's that way,' she muttered, waving a crooked arm to a door in the far corner. So he probably missed the grey suede walls and ankle-deep coffee carpets.

He undressed her flat body. Her skin was white, veined with blue, and around the scoop of her hips, her bones stuck out like crater edges on the moon. She moaned with impatience. She had waited for this moment for thirty-three years. She had planned it. The drink would get her through it. Don was quick – grateful he could manage anything with the amount of drink he'd consumed. And, as he made love to her, she realised that this was not what she thought it was all about. The wonders of sex were no more than an ugly heaving and squelching and a lot of pain. Nobody ever mentioned the pain. All the eavesdropping years, listening to the girls, watching as they prinked in front of mirrors with heated tongs, balanced on steep stilettos, all so they would be attractive to have sex – for that! The dream of losing her virginity had crumpled like the skins of burst party balloons.

The next morning, Don crept out of the flat. He tried to touch the bony back wrapped in a man's dressing gown, but she shook off his affection, concentrating her gaze on the bluish screen of her laptop. At work, nothing was mentioned between them, and, over the following weeks, the story of Miss Cliff and the office party floated into the ether of office mythology. Paulette returned to her comforting rows of figures, her leather chairs and *a bloody good glass of wine*.

She failed to observe that her periods had stopped. They were such a damn inconvenience and always irregular. She'd picked up some sort of bug, she thought as she retched, head in the bowl of her toilet - legs akimbo - green in the hollows of her cheeks.

'Congratulations Miss Cliff. Well well. What very good news.' The doctor pulled off a pair of disposable gloves with a crack as Paulette straightened her legs. 'You have no family do you? Is there anyone?'

Paulette, dressing behind the screen, thought of her mother in another world, dipped in the mists of Prozac and gin, and her brothers with their families and their friendly wives.

'No,' she said, 'no one.'

As she sped back to her flat, ignoring the seven speed cameras on her route, her thoughts were wild. She remembered Denise on the second floor, the growing bump, and her PA's remarks. 'Poor girl, she'll find it hard to manage. Her bloke's done a runner... heard about the baby and went off just like that... still, she's got her Mum.'

The view of the Thames failed to console her. She yanked the heavy curtain pull, shutting out the other world of river, buildings and lights. Grabbed a bottle of wine, poured a large glass, and kicked off the practical court-shoes.

She could pay for an abortion, although she had left it rather late. There might be medical objections. Or she could have the thing. Anger raged. She pulled at her clothes, discarding them in a pile at her feet and began to pluck at her board-flat belly, sobbing. Damn it. She was crying. She never cried. Not since...

Three crisp white men's shirts saw her through her pregnancy together with two strangely constructed pairs of maternity trousers with pouch stomachs. *Looks like I'm giving birth to a bloody kangaroo*, she thought.

But at the end of her ninth month, during a meeting with the suits upstairs, she began to feel twinges. They increased with the volume of the chairman's voice. When the meeting was over she decided to take a taxi to the hospital.

The midwives had seen it all before – the terrified ones, the hopeful ones and the ones who didn't want. They closed their ears to her fury and, finally, after twenty-four hours of swearing and screaming, Paulette gave a desperate last push accompanied by a curse; and a bloody lump slithered into the hands of the joyful midwives.

'It's a little girl!' they chorused.

They rested the child – eyes wide-awake blue – on Paulette's flat breasts.

'She's lovely,' cooed the first midwife. 'And a wonderful healthy weight – seven and a half pounds. Born on the first hour of May. Have you decided yet what to call her?'

'No!' glowered Paulette, returning the child to the midwife. 'You name her if you want.'

The midwife's mouth opened. Then choked. 'I know it's a bit bewildering. But you'll soon love her. She's so pretty. Why don't you call her May, until you think of something yourself?'

'Fine,' said Paulette and turned her back.

The nurses and midwives took pity on May, feeding her when necessary, and the hospital psychiatrist was alerted. He talked to Paulette about her feelings for the child. And to protect herself from his army of social workers, she feigned interest.

When she returned home it took only a minute on the Internet, and clothes, Moses basket, pram, feeding bottles, nappies and baby-wipes were purchased. Paulette planned a return to her previous life. May lived an infancy of pass the parcel, moving from the office crèche to the ministrations of a part-time housekeeper and her PA's daughter Sally who had always liked babies and was short of money. Her needs were haphazardly taken care of; if she required a new coat or new shoes, whoever was in charge at the time would buy the item. But the child thrived, with a sunny nature, and even loved her mother, despite her mother's apparent lack of interest.

It was the end of April, approaching her fourth birthday. May had attended kindergarten that morning and her teacher had told them a story about fairies. All her friends had seen fairies because they had gardens. May was convinced that fairies couldn't fly up so many floors to a flat like hers, especially in the city. But she hoped that maybe if she wore a fairy outfit, they might see her and want to be her friend.

Paulette was tucking her into bed trying to see if she could shave away a few minutes of May's quality time to study figures for the next day's meeting.

'Mummy, can I have a fairy outfit for my birthday with silver shoes... and... and, maybe a party?' whispered May, pulling Paulette towards her face for a good night kiss.

'We'll see.' Paulette shut her face, thinking of the waste of an outfit and the effort of purchase. She'd mentally moved into the leather chair with the glass of red, as she covered the child's shoulders with her quilt.

Damn nuisance. She doesn't have to have that... I haven't got the time...

Hours later, the phone jangled hollow, through the flat.

Late for someone to ring?

'Paul, Paul, Hi... Sorry to ring so late... it's Mum, I'm afraid. She's gone... I've only got down here myself... Paul, Paul... Are you there?

'Yes... yes. Was it bad?'

'Well, it had been getting worse for years... you know that... but the end was quick... heart attack, the doctor said. You will come down, won't you?'

Paulette sank on the floor, the phone cable tangled around her bony wrist.

'Yes, I'll be there,' she answered weakly.

Bernice's body was quickly dispatched, without flowers as requested. Donations to Cancer Research. Back at the house, Paulette's rugby-playing brothers sat, still in their dark suits, large hands holding dainty sandwiches and tiny liqueur glasses. Paulette felt the urge to laugh. She was never very good at social occasions.

'I'll go up to the loft and get out the Will,' she murmured.

She pushed open the door of the loft and clambered up, sneezing and clawing at chains of webs clinging to her face. A small chest sat tucked in the corner, behind a broken chair and the boys' Tonka trucks, with its own layer of dust. It was unlocked. Inside, a pile of yellowing deeds lay sleeping. As Paulette pulled them from their resting place, two small snapshots fell out. One was of her, her mother and the boys on holiday somewhere, all in shorts smiling with ice creams. The other was a picture of a child dressed in a long green dress with Wellington boots.

She held the picture close to her spectacled face. Looked at the golden curls, the puzzled smile.

'May!' she cried.

WASN'T THAT A DAINTY DISH...?

The moment he'd rung and said that he was coming home for the weekend – home to me – I started to plan and dream. I must be crazy. Thoughts, jumping like fleas: erratic, list-making crazy moments suffused with elation and despair, rolling the months back like shedding tired cardigans and fitting back into the neat, trim fitted T-shirts of my past. God, he hated sloppiness. No time for a diet, but time for hair-colour, underarm wax, a full leg-wax and bikini wax – ouch.

All done, the day after I scrubbed the house, including the corners – all those bits where grime seems to lurk, just behind the door in the bathroom, under the wash basin. I jammed odd letters and trivia into rattan boxes, stood the books – now shiny-jacketed – regimental straight and hid the girly teddies, substituting one orchid in a green glass bowl on the coffee table – enigmatic, suggesting a confident persona, hopefully my new image. Gradually, with each task, my thoughts became more focused, more positive.

Until I thought of the girls' reactions. I could hear them. 'You must be mad... you're a bloody fool even letting him back for a chat, after the way... 'There's Claire tossing her Nicky Clark-type bob, muttering, 'you're too good for him girl... move on, plenty more... fish, frogs, princes... ' And Zena, worse. 'I don't know how you can talk to him after all those times... even he's told you he's been with others... you're just cheapening yourself... '

But I have to give it a chance. There's never been anyone else. Anyone.

Sometimes I'll sit in the quiet of the pub snug, right in the corner, or in a restaurant where the suits like to go, and watch them: other men. Imagine that one of them is mine. I've played the game watching a male voice choir perform. There they are, standing stiffly, rows of men, forcing their mouths wide open, carefully forming syllables and consonants, eyes concentrating on a spot on the horizon. How about that one, or that one? Would I fancy the one with the florid complexion and the freckles... would he be any more faithful than mine...? There's always the chance... it was good once, wasn't it?

We first met in Uni. I was working in the bar for a bit of extra cash. I remember how he walked over to me crinkle-eyed, with a second-hand Homburg from Oxfam half-pulled over his face, covering a thicket of curls, trying to look sophisticated. I saw him and loved him. Simple as that. He must have felt the same because after that we were inseparable. We have three children, for goodness sake! Then one night as we are going to bed he announces that he's not in love with me any more. That he's in love with another. Like a B movie or an American serial – a Dallas. Not my man and our relationship. Infidelity. What's that? The interloper that creeps into my house, into his head and steals my husband from me with false smiles and a perfect nubile body. I saw her once in slim, pale jeans and hair deftly pleated into a chignon. She does exist. I thought she had a hard face. But dare I be bitchy? As I looked at her I felt old. Well, I am older. Dressed in the skin of a mature woman. Not as trim or as pert in parts, though not bad. Besides, he said he loved my body, with all its imperfections. He'd kiss the gap between my neck and shoulder and tell me that was Eden. Behind my knees... smooth my ankles. He'd talk of my downy skin... of my perfume... Our love-making was good.

But now I'm set in my ways, the girls say. More like a trapped insect fossilized in amber. Rigid within my needs. And the truth of it is I don't really want another – want in either way, emotionally or biblically. I want him. Even though he's moved away. Perhaps the whole episode was a male menopause thing – that last burst when the fears of men erupt, and they panic that their sexual life is draining out of them. She was just a diversion. He's told me it's all over. I want to believe him. I have to give him one more chance. If only for the memories. His crazy food fancies. His desire for elegant Japanese food, perfectly arranged in fine porcelain bowls, and, an hour later, his craving for chips in Caroline Street. Or Mars-Bar-man, two giant bars, one after another, then mozzarella cheese cut thick with beef tomatoes, sprinkled with chopped basil and freshly milled black pepper. Like the incongruous mix that was him.

The house has never looked so beautiful. Outside, as if helping me welcome him home, the first pink-tipped candles on the magnolia are just breaking out of their green holders. And the pots I managed to fill in between tears are full of crocuses and daffodils.

This afternoon I made the food. This has to be the best meal I have ever prepared. I thought I might make my own sushi to start and then I thought that looked too much like trying – keep to something elegant but straightforward. His favourites. So I filled two brandy glasses with cut peeled cucumber, pieces of Ogen melon, and peeled kiwis, sharpened with the juice and finely grated rind of a lemon and loads of chopped mint. I decorated them with a spoonful of Greek yogurt and a slice of lemon and mint leaf and popped them in the fridge ready to serve. I prepared pancakes, filled with pine-nuts, chestnuts and wild mushrooms in a red wine sauce, with Moroccan carrots and a crisp green salad. And for dessert – though I was hoping we might not get there – I made some sharp fresh mango and raspberry sorbet with his favourite vanilla biscuits and coffee – good, good coffee.

I laid the table with pale-green serviettes and a vase of the first primroses out of the garden with a few sprigs of pussy-willow. Lit candles spread a luminous glow over the table and a bottle of his Frascati sat waiting in the fridge. I'd even made the bread he loved so much – studded with green and black olives and scented with rosemary.

Then, a fragrant bath – all ready. New dress, very high stilettos. The ones that pinch as you walk but look good. A spray of Miracle on every part of my body. Oh God... Oh God... Dear Lord. Please make it all better. Let him come back. Let him *want* to come back.

The familiar feet at the door. The cave from my belly to my chest is full of crawling insects. My hands shaking. It's raining fine needles. He pulls off his coat, shaking it away from his body like a wet dog, and tosses it on the newly washed cream covers of the couch. I would have said something in the past... not this time. Perhaps I can pretend he's returning from work as usual. Like he was never away. Hold back. Don't appear too eager.

'Hello, Mike, you must be soaked.'

'I'm fine.'

'Good journey? It's... it's awful weather.' Dear Lord, such pathetic language... the words I want to say are trapped inside me. 'I'll get you a drink... a whisky or a beer?'

'Yes, beer sounds good.'

I go into the kitchen to get out a beer, from the four I've left chilling in the fridge. He's walking round the house, opening cupboards, running his hands over the surfaces of the mahogany shelves he installed for me. We had such an argument over those bookshelves. I wanted antique wood bought from the salvage yard. He was tired, said the DIY stuff, stained up, would look just as good. But in the end, he agreed that the salvage yard timber would look so much better. Now he's moved over to the fireplace, trailing fingers over the polished silver frames of the children – our children – and the few remaining photos of his late parents. He's like a blind person using Braille to translate the past. Now, at this moment, I'm sorry we didn't take his mother's Bergere suite from his family home, rather than buy the three piece suite. He did want to keep it. But it didn't match the room, all that dark carved wood and woven cane. Besides, it was far too large.

In a minute, maybe he'll see me... really see me.

'Are you managing OK?'

'Yes... yes.' My words falter. He's always been a good provider. Even that night, straight after, there was money. He left two hundred pounds in twenties lying on the bed, on my white linen sheets, wrapped in a beige elastic band.

'And the children are ...?'

'Yes, yes... no problem at all.'

He wanted them to go to the local comp. But I believed that private education would give them the best start in life, the same as my parents had given me, and so we both worked harder to pay for their schooling. 'Self-inflicted poverty,' he'd mutter, if there was another school trip, new football boots, or a change in the uniform. I used to dread the letters in the end. But we'd carry on, just more tired in the evenings and maybe more irritable. Still, that was a long time ago and Sally is in London now working in PR, and Huw has worked with the same estate agents since leaving after his O levels.

I want to touch him. Slip my hand in his. Feel his warm body lean against mine until we melt into one. But I'm afraid.

At last the courage to look at his face – the face I love. It's his face but the expression is odd. I reach over to touch his arm, but he ignores the gesture. Then his eyes walk over my table, the laid glasses, the lit candle, the flowers. He studies my arrangement. I stand there, waiting, hoping. Then he looks at me. Expressionless, the features that I loved chiseled into rock, rigid. The large brown loving eyes chilled into glitter-glass, like a lump of slag from the iron works at Cyfarthfa.

'Glass of wine?' I say. He's finished the beer.

'Maybe.'

I try to tell him with my eyes how I still love him, how I want him. I try to touch his hand when I pass the wine-glass but he pulls away. He pulls out one of the dining room chairs and sits on that, pushing away a laid knife, fork, and side-plate, so that he can use the tablemat to rest his glass, then turns his body away from the table and my preparations.

'Dinner?' I ask.

'Wine is fine for the moment, thanks.'

I sit the bottle next to him. He drinks quickly, nervously filling glass after glass. Time laughs behind my back as the salad wilts.

'Shall we eat?' I try again.

He turns round. Studies the liquid in his glass, swirling it round and round in a greasy rotatation, before laying it down, slowly. Then he casts a tired eye over my preparations and looks straight at me. 'I'm not coming back. I thought, perhaps it was possible. But the minute I came back in the house I knew it was wrong. Look at it... You're so immaculate. So perfect... I can't take it... '

THE PINK DEVORÉ SKIRT

I'd promised to go to town with my daughter. She finds it difficult to get out with a new baby and she'd managed to get a sitter for a few hours.

'You are coming aren't you, Mum?'

'Yes... yes, of course love...'

'I've been so looking forward. Is there something wrong?'

'No love... no. Of course there isn't.'

I couldn't tell her. He'd made me swear not to say, just two days before, when we sat together on our bench in the park. Wrapped in fleeces, hats and gloves we shivered in the pale midday light. Ice smoke blew from our mouths. We sat pretending it was summer. A flock of greylags crowded our quiet. But we'd forgotten the bread. Custom interrupted by other thoughts.

'But I need to say. I'll have to talk. I don't think I can do this on my own.' I whispered.

233

'It wouldn't be right... suppose there was nothing. The doctor said that until these tests are completed, we won't really know. She's only just getting over postnatal depression... It's not fair to give her that sort of worry.'

We meet in the coffee shop where words of trivia are thrown away with the bam-bam music and the throaty choke of the coffee machine. She looks so lovely, our kid, the new mum, constantly worried about a belly – a small legacy from a difficult pregnancy and birth. He's right. I can't say. But I have always been so close to my daughter. It would be good to share the problem.

'Mum, you're so quiet... a hot drink? That'll make you feel better. I'll go and get it. It's most probably that bout of 'flu you've just had.'

I must make an effort. I'm such a bloody awful liar. She goes to get the drinks and I'm grateful for a few moments of calm to pacify the bad that churns around in my throat and rides switchback to my stomach. I make a quick exit to the toilet to wash my eyes. As I re-do them with a smear of over-bright silver and taupe, I can hear my dead parents' derisive voices. *We told you he was far too old for you. But you had to marry him didn't you? We said one day you'd be sorry.*

I never saw him as older. Just kinder – more considerate. I never noticed any difference between us. In fact, at the end of May, when we walked the dogs through the violet mist of bluebells near our home, solid walking boots sinking into moist mushroomy humus, I was the one who asked to slow down, panting and giggling. He moved on quicker, advancing, turning round to joke, face crumpled with laughter.

234

Then turned round to come back to me, to make sure I was alright.

Sarah and I sit on commodious brown leather couches with alien sounds thudding from a nearby CD player and I swallow too quickly, scalding my throat. The small buttery biscuit that accompanies – the treat of the week – is consumed in two bites whereas I usually make it last for the whole of the drink. In my mind the words revolve:

Darling, You know that Grandpa had prostate cancer... well the doctor thought... we both thought... we thought it would be best if Dad had the test... so many millions to one, but as a safety precaution... best to know. The results were not... not as we hoped...

I can't even discuss them in my mind but I need, I want, to talk. I have to name the devils that derange my equilibrium. Right now, just trying to converse with my daughter and not say the words that are foremost in my mind demands supreme effort. Ask about the baby – discuss feeds and waking up in the night and how her figure is not returning to its former elastic shape, and... that bloody awful subject sits hovering above us, mocking.

'Mum, I reckon it's a bit of retail therapy that's necessary. Haven't you got that do to go to?'

I haul out one of my jokey smiles and pretend.

'Good lord, yes. Jan's wedding.'

The need for something special for my best friend's daughter's wedding now seems like the Joker, a card tossed by a malignant magician.

'It's that 'flu... Let's go and have a mooch round the shops and then ask Dad if he minds a scratch supper and you put your feet up a bit.'

If Dad minds – that's the thing. He has never minded, especially about food. He has always been the kindest man I know. Gentle, undemanding, just as happy with a piece of cheese and a bit of bread as a grand dinner. He's always said 'whatever's easiest'.

We are pushing past the shopping crowds that blur before my eyes. Bellies out, protruding and pierced... why is it the ones that shouldn't, do? My path is assaulted by push chairs laden with crying children, steered by mothers who ignore their howls, and elderly men who seem to have lost their way and walk stiffly without purpose.

Can't you see, love, I really don't care? Nothing matters. I just want your Dad to be alright.

She's urging me into shops laden with bright colours and then we find it. It's shimmering, hanging with a row of others. A soft plum-coloured Devoré skirt embroidered with oriental roses and silky dark green leaves. I love it for the sheer exuberance of its design. My daughter forces me to try it on and both my daughter and the shop assistant make cooing noises of approbation. In a daze I buy, thinking, if I acquire this skirt, will I spoil his chances? Be tempting fate?

His face has been with me throughout the purchase. I keep seeing him in his gardening outfit, gentle with seeds and plants, a face like a loving father when he's growing things. Will we go to that wedding or will that glorious skirt sit unused and forlorn in the wardrobe, while he endures the grimness of chemo and radiography?

A few days ago, we had the result of my three yearly mammogram. My hand shook as I recognised the address.

'We are pleased to inform you...'

Why wasn't it me rather than him? I need it to be me. Women can cope – they are used to pain. The skirt is wrapped in pink tissue paper and we leave the shop and my daughter is so pleased for me. 'You'll look lovely in that and you had to get something special. Dad will love it.'

Can I show it to him? Is he going to think that by buying something for a wedding in a few months time I am being insensitive?

Two weeks later the consultant called him to his office. I sat outside in the bland motel-like consulting room fighting my worst thoughts. But we were lucky. We were safe. I wore the skirt and we partied. After a battery of painful tests, the results were that the enlarged growth was benign. Our lives could spin again on their insecure axis, protected, we hoped, by our prayers and the relief that for now we had been given permission by some greater force, to write in diaries, make plans, think of holidays. But in our minds, an invisible wire would tie us fast and, every six months, wind us back to the tune of terror.

Now my daughter is expecting her next child. She rests on the couch watching our granddaughter who is now two and a half. Sitting on a footstool with chubby legs extended under a low side table, the little one carefully spoons my bright orange carrot soup into her mouth and dips granary bread into her Fimbles bowl. I've started to let her manage on her own even though the odd drop plops on the floor. I cherish the blonde silken curls caught back into butterfly clips, and her young child's profile, concentrating on the task of coping.

Such a pretty child and so affectionate, I think. She's getting very good at feeding herself. I'm lucky to have her so close to me... to us.

The phone rings.

'Love, it's...'

'I'll take it outside.'

I know from the tenor of our GP's voice that the news is bad. Just a few days ago my husband went for his blood test. I'll have to keep the confidence again. It's that same routine – where the secrets sit in our minds. Never on our lips.

That night we go to bed and make love – and it is special and wonderful, but now, when we rest, linked as one, in the easy comfort of bodies that have lived together for almost thirty five years, we keep inside our private words. Hold them fast to ourselves. If they say that he is ill and he has treatment and it works, will he recover, or will he perhaps have to be content to be, in his eyes, a lesser man? A man walking with the cruelties of drugs and their side-effects. How could I comfort him, so proud of his abilities, his successes, if he lost any part of his life? I start the silent mantra of prayers. *If I promise to do everything I can to observe the practices of my religion, to try even harder... please... please... can he be...*

Eventually, he falls asleep and the unspoken words lie on my pillow. I go down and make cups of tea and sit at the computer hoping I can work at something and obtain temporary relief. The house is shivering cold at three in the morning and the dark outside watches me and gives me no comfort. The words bounce on the screen. At last I see the dawn filter shades of violet onto the black, and I return to my bed. Half-asleep he calls, 'You OK, love?'

'Yes, fine.'

He turns his shoulder and settles. The bird chorus and the sounds of morning become my consolation. Strange how the sounds of the ordinary – the electric whine of the milk-float and the clatter of bottles, early motorists, their tyres whooshing through the autumn puddles – can be so supporting. Everything's the same – he's next to me, so we'll be all right. Oh, to be an ostrich. In those couple of hours before he wakes, I run through the memory of our life together: afraid I might forget and not hold the precious links of our shared time: like a broken cinema production, blanks of reality and then back to the past how we met, how he proposed. How I was upset when he didn't do the whole on-the-knee stuff, but in the back of his Morris 1100, with Andy Williams playing easy listening. And how he just looked at me, thin, very thin and young, with laughter dancing on the crinkles of his eyes,

'I suppose we'd better get married then. What do you think?'

I teased him for years. 'Suppose, suppose?' And the birth of our children and the bad days when parents died. Oh yes the damn *d* word that we hide, walk past, avoid, it's always there. It's always there like a greedy beast sucking out our sanity.

Later in the day we walk with our dogs, a security ritual, an escape from our fears. It's November and the most beautiful autumn I can remember. Above us stretch blue skies hung with skeins of white. Our dogs pull on the leads and their noses twitch with the longings of the chase, as young squirrels run across our path. The copper beeches' brocade-rich gold and russet bend with their load of rain-slicked leaves. We move past the lake and find the rose gardens still heavy with the scent of roses and we stand resting for seconds amazed at summer which still sits in this sunny spot.

'Who could possibly predict that we could still see roses, unblemished, in November – that's amazing, isn't it?' he says and we bury our noses in velvet petals and breathe their rich scents.

'Let's go out for a bit of supper,' he says. 'Just you and me, and wear your special skirt, the one you bought for Jan's wedding, I always liked that skirt.' He never knew how I stood in that shop and worried about the consequences of the purchase. How our futures focussed within those delicate weaves of warp and weft.

And I stand in the park with the liquid sound of a single robin in the background. Autumn trees surround me, some of them. still green, and I realise that we must go on even though our life-span is unknown. All predictions can be wrong. No-one has total understanding of our expectations. What we have is sweet, precious and worth the fight.

PATCHWORK

They have confined me to a hospital bed. They think I am ill. But they are wrong. I am happy, content within my cell-like withdrawal. The alabaster whiteness of the walls and the bleached linen of the sheets have created a perfect cocoon. There is no sink, no toilet. Nothing where I can eliminate, evacuate. But I have my ways. The nurse in charge of me is not vigilant. She uses my toilet time to phone her friends. So far I have been lucky.

Every day a doctor comes to visit me. Although he's a he, he is not a man. He just wears man's clothes and a starched ivory coat – a bloodless arrangement of person with a stethoscope around an anaemic neck and pewter grey hair. He is accompanied by a nurse, brings weighing scales and talks to me of food, of eating, of gaining weight, of the outside world, of my need to join these people. But I have no such desires.

241

Some days a window cleaner washes the outside contaminated glass of my window. He is a man. I watch him as I lie in my bed. I see the tight T-shirt pulled over muscled shoulders; the arms etched with dark hairs, ligaments roped like strong twine, pushing a chamois over the glass. He pretends that he does not see me. He is told to keep his eyes averted.

I have brought my patchwork. It projects my mind away from their constant nagging and uses up a few calories. I was going to cut the pieces here. I would enjoy watching the silver steel of my tailor's knife lacerate and cleave seams carefully sewn. But they found the scissors concealed in my bag and removed them. I suppose they thought I might do something with the blade. Close with a suicide's bracelet? They do not understand.

I was allowed to bring the pieces ready cut. My mother supervised the preparation. She said that it would not be good, not be perfect, for all the fabrics are different and for a patchwork quilt each fabric has to be of equal density and of similar type. But flawlessness is not the object of the making. She always needs the ideal, always striving for the unattainable that I, too, am supposed to crave. I like to mix the colours palette bright in my colourless cell, lying on my blanched bedcovers. They vibrate with their own violent energies.

I start with my brown cotton striped school dress. They do not understand the pleasure I derive slicing and bruising the fabric. There is a smell about it – a damp, sweaty chalky mix of cooked cabbage and fecund bodies. The carved wooden panels ache with the fears of the inadequate. Ink-splotched desks hold their young captives prisoner. 'We expect you to do

242

well. We did not have all your advantages. Your mother and I were lucky to get out when the rest of the family perished. We have had to work, save, and sacrifice for you to get to that school.'

Cut it with knives. Blade its existence. Sew it into something that is mine. My design – perfectly imperfect.

Royal Blue is the uniform towel from my school showers – a nauseous smell of chlorine, foot dip and cheap deodorants. 'Please Miss. I can't do games this week. Can I be excused? Can I be excused showers?' The cream and dark green tiled walls shiver with the echoes of the misunderstood. I have developed early. I am a full-breasted woman with a mid-European bone structure, solid, heavy. My nipples are tight, erect with fear. Lithesome girls with tight, tiny breasts nudge each other, giggle behind my back. Some are staring. I run my fingers over the harsh terry cloth. 'It will spoil the patchwork,' my mother says. But it has to be executed. Cut it. Make it into pieces. It has lost its life.

Yellow is the seersucker tablecloth from my home. It lay on the kitchen table listening to the murmuring of the ancient fridge and the constant bubbling of a pot on the stove. Sometimes it is chicken soup, steaming with golden carrots, onions, and celery, creamy barley and beans, or green pea soup so thick we would joke about having a slice for supper. My mother's tiny green glass vase from her first life sat on that cloth. It had been wrapped in a peasant shawl with her candlesticks and a few photographs when she ran. I'm sorry I broke it. Yellow is the cadmium colour of the wallpaper of my bedroom, of golden egg yolks and rich butter, of sticky dried apricots chopped with peel and moist bananas crushed with the zesty juices and rinds of sharp, knobbly lemons. Whip them together. Beat in the sugar. Fold in the soft white flour. Make a cake for Daddy for his tea. Not for me.

Pink is the nylon tulle dress from my Barbie. 'Why do you have to have such a doll? We never had such dolls in the old country. Such a strange birthday present for a child of thirteen!' But she is perfect. She is beautiful. She is thin with long, blond silky hair, shapely breasts, no stomach and no sex hair. I want to be her. She makes it impossible. Cut her dress. Finish it.

Purple is the colour of my cheap Lycra bathing costume. We sit together – a day at the seaside. But the parents keep their clothes on. My father rolls up his black trouser legs exposing white skin and blue, cabled veins. My mother unbuttons her blouse a little. I see creases in her breasts. She looks at my father. They laugh and then, a little uncomfortable, they look at me. My mother's face goes pink. I do not like the feeling. I do not like the look my Uncle Saul gives me when I have to relinquish my towel from around my body, to run into the sea. Though when I am away from them, it is beautiful. I taste the smack of the wind hitting my face, the fingers of the warm sun, touching, loving, unconditional. But then I have to return. To Uncle Saul's eyes smirring over my body, through the stretchy costume to my secret places. Cut into slivers with the honed silver steel. It curls as it cuts. Decimate its existence.

Mamma does not fuss as we slice my old pinafore into neat squares. The background is cream with tiny green and pink flowers. Though she does not see *why* it has to go. It saves the good clothes... always save... keep for best. Help Mamma in the kitchen. We have to cook a special meal. Uncle Saul is coming for supper. Mamma is excited. *Gefilte* fish to start – fluffy, poached balls of fish lying cold on glass plates decorated with a slice of carrot. Then *borscht*, soup the colour of blood... 'Grate the beetroot darling. Uncle Saul loves a good soup.' Then Mamma takes the boiling chicken that has flavoured the soup and sets it in a casserole to brown with rice in its bed and more carrots. Dessert is my job. 'Make the pastry. You have such a light hand.' I enjoy rubbing the sticky margarine into the flour with a little vanilla sugar, and seeing the whole come to a pliant ball with lemon and egg. Mamma has gone upstairs to wash and change. Uncle Saul comes early. I have just finished putting the sliced apples into the pie with cinnamon and sultanas. I am putting the pastry on the top. I used to love the smell of cinnamon. Now I hate it. Cut up the apron. Get rid of its face.

Red is the colour of my best Shabbat dress, now a year old. I love its sleek velvet fabric and the garnet colour is reminiscent of autumn light through the synagogue stained-glass windows. It is Friday night – the highlight of the week. We sit around the solid dining room table laid with the best snowy, damask cloth. The polished silver candlesticks bear ivory candles; they cast a gentle flickering luminance over the waiting family. The *kiddush* cups have been polished bright and two vast crusty *challot* sit under their white embroidered cover waiting for my father's blessing. He trickles the blood-coloured liquid into the silver *bechas*. It is one of my favourite sounds. We stand for *kiddush* – the Sabbath blessing. As we rise, the white pearly buttons on my dress pop, exposing my new bra. My little brother giggles and my father mutters something to my mother about me developing and having a suitable dress for a woman, not a child. But I do not want...

Grey is the colour of my father's face. I have no fabric for his face. I hear him talking to the doctor outside my door – hushed sounds not words.

My mother is upset that I want to cut all these materials. 'It is a waste to cut up good things. They could be passed on and I could sell the red dress,' she says. But the doctor is on my side and says they have to indulge me. When he visited me this time, he wanted to examine my body. As he pulled back my nightdress, revealing my shrunken breasts and bloated stomach, he discovered the belt from my red dress pulled tight about my waist. 'What is this here for?' he said gently, as if talking to a small child. 'It keeps me safe,' I whispered. I dare not tell him that every day I pull it a bit tighter. It stops my appetite. 'But it is stopping your blood,' he said in his sing-song voice. Yes, my blood has stopped, the other blood, the woman's blood. When the doctor goes, his face too is grey like my father's. I pull off my nightdress and look at my body. There is no mirror in my room. It is not allowed. They say that I am thin – that I could lose my life, but I only see fat, bulges of blubber poured into skin, covered by a soft fluffy down.

My father returns. He has talked to the doctor. He says that if I would eat a little, I can go on a long holiday to Italy. Sit in the sun. Drink coffee in a dusty piazza. Lie in a chair watching mists clear over slate-blue mountains with tall cypresses standing on tiptoe for a better view, listen to cicadas sounding like old wristwatches being rewound, and gentle bird song in vast magnolia trees.

I am going to try to eat. My father's grey face upsets me too much. I do not want to hurt him.

*   *   *

I am sitting at the side of a glittering lake. Small ochre and terracotta-coloured buildings cleave to gentle slopes and the sounds of clinking church bells bless the sunlit landscape. The colours of my patchwork have found new meaning.

The brown and white striped cotton has been pin-tucked and transformed into an arch of reeds at the edge of the lake safe-keeping grebes, mallards and a flotilla of swans. Beneath, below its ankles, rainbows of small fish arrow through craggy shards of granite and marble.

Blue is the lake water – navy and turquoise wrinkled silk sprinkled with sequins of sunlight basted to a muslin sky and pinned and tacked by tiny pen–and-ink sailing boats.

Yellow are the fields of sunflowers, rough cloth of *girasole* that point their seeded heads to the warming sun, and fields of maize, their spires golden as they ripen and climb to the light.

Pink is the polished marble of Verona. We feel its hardness and its history at our feet as we walk. Pink is also the colour of soft tulle sunsets on the lake when the sun is tired and waits for the silver attendance of the moon.

Purple is embroidered bougainvillea, hugging sunlit loggias with violet passion. And freckles of tiny scabious and wild cyclamen decorating, petit point, the hedgerows and cool, shady woods where blackberries and blueberries wait for the plucking.

My apron is now a sunlit meadow of light cotton organza which holds its summer flowers outstretched to the light. It is the host to ancient olive trees spreading convoluted branches, legend-telling as they sit and wait for another harvest.

My colour red is still wine, but not the bloody, fortified stuff of religion. It is the light pourings of crushed grapes tasting of warm vineyards and laughter. Red is also the colour of my new cotton sundress. My mother is pleased. She tells me it is a good shape and that I look better.

My father has lost the grey from his face. He makes jokes with my mother and from time to time I see him look at me. They think that I am cured and this makes them happy.

Except Italy has given me a new way of living. I have discovered a way to eat which keeps them and me contented. They see me eat pasta with rich tomato sauces. Relish pizzas crisp out of fire-baked ovens, lick ice creams made of crushed strawberries folded with whipped cream, feast on peaches and nectarines from gentle orchards.

But now I have discovered a trick. It is a conspiracy between my two fingers, the back of my throat and my stomach. I eat my whole meal. They watch and smile at each other. At the end of the meal, I make myself excused and then it is done – a couple of minutes and all is eliminated. It is easy to check that everything is out. At last, I can taste and eat all the things I would never allow myself. Sometimes I eat just for the eating. I force down cold pasta waiting for tomorrow's sauces, ice cream and chocolate till my body will burst with the forcing. In the black velvet when they are asleep with only the rhythm of the fridge playing its music, I stuff... gorge... lust after food. But my woman's blood has not, will not, return.

*   *   *

We are home. Italy is past. Smudgy grey skies saturated with ice skewers of rain make stabbing autumn sounds on the outside of the house. They talk of my education. I must go back to school. I do not want to be with those people. Tomorrow Uncle Saul and Aunty Millie will eat with us. He is here now, staying the night, as he wants to go to our synagogue tomorrow morning with my father. We have been busy all day preparing a special meal for *Rosh Hashono* – the Jewish New Year. In the fridge are two fat balls of pastry, resting, waiting for me to attend to them. The one pastry is a light short crust that I have to make into a pie; the other is richer for biscuits.

All last night, I lay on my bed immobile, rigid with fear. It is now early morning and I cannot stay in my room. I need to eat to drown the furies. But I have to be careful now I am home. They watch me all the time. The doctor has warned them. He is suspicious about my condition – my little conjuring trick. As I walk down the stairs I feel my heart banging in my throat. My body shakes. My stomach is screaming. I go to the fridge door. What can I take? There is a whole chicken, intact – I can't touch that. We have made *knaidlech* – small dumplings to boil in the soup. I push them in my mouth, raw salty dough, putting others together so that they will not detect any disappearances. I go to the cupboards. Cereal, raw cereal without milk, dry so that it makes me cough; fingers in golden syrup, strings sticky over my body.

249

Faster, faster, two lumps of pastry. I cut pieces and force it in without tasting. My heart beats so fast. I feel dizzy and faint. I sink to the floor. The black and white ceramic tiles are cool to my throbbing, bloated, overheated body. I look across at the dog's bowl. My mother has put the spare pieces of meat from the soup flavouring into it. The dog has had enough. I look around. My father will be down soon. The day is about to start. The pieces of meat in the dog's bowl lie calling me. I take the bowl and force greasy pieces of meat into my mouth.

There is a sound at the door and Uncle Saul walks into the kitchen wearing an old faded silk dressing gown. I see his face drawn with horror.

OUT OF THE BLUE

I am sitting on a balcony overlooking a garden in Marrakech. 'Having a wonderful time' would be the postcard cliché. The water in the small pool is blue, fed by six glittering fountains, and above, a large Moroccan lamp set with lapis lazuli coloured glass swings gently in a faint breeze. The air is bubbling with the generous serenades of nightingales calling to mates and the booming of soft pink and beige collar doves. Swallows scythe the sky, cutting figure-of-eight silhouettes in the golden sunset. We have just eaten a perfect supper of fresh salads, curls of lettuce and a frizz of wild roquette, tomatoes as big as a child's finger, eggs laid by chickens who have roamed hot farmyards scratching the dusty ground. A spicy couscous jewelled with vegetables followed, and a light dessert of rice pudding fragrant with rosewater and almonds completed, with mint tea and a platter of fruits still holding their dewy bloom from local orchards.

My husband dozes now, 'Just forty winks', while I turn on BBC Television World News. His breath rises and falls, lullaby gentle, while I drink mint tea and revel in my holiday freedom. I am beginning to get to grips with a novel I have been writing for three years. It has been an arduous task. Based on events of the Holocaust, and family recollections, the research has been fraught with anguish and pain. I have probed the contents of book-shops, libraries, The Imperial War Museum. My fingers have travelled dry sheets with blood written on their pages. I have been the inquisitor. How many dead? Ten thousand here, twenty thousand... a million there, interred in references. But I can cope. I understand. The books are haunted with ghosts, with mutilations, tortures. But it is the written word. I can cope with a written agony. There is a level of detachment which allows me to enquire and relate and retain my sanity. The word is my world.

And I am fortunate. I am the next generation. I have never suffered the fear of war, of being persecuted for my beliefs. Yes, in school, there were those who... Well, if it wasn't because of that... So many are bullied. I know these groups exist. The people who hate my type. And it is because of them that we have to have security to meet and to pray, but even that is moderated by the tolerance of the majority.

I go inside and watch the World Service. I catch the end first. Tim Henman has been beaten again. A cyclist has been pushed off the road in competition, by one of the motorcycle outriders. Now the news. A group of Latvian war criminals has been released without trial... forgiven. The newsreel runs on. Black and white pictures flicker slightly, filmed by Nazis proud of their success. The announcer's voice is matter of fact. In a minute he will speak of Africa and the financial situation in America.

My husband sleeps softly. In my present, in the now of my life, I am in this room drinking mint tea, watching television. This is my holiday. This morning we visited scented palaces reminiscent of Ali Baba, studded with minute tiles that shimmered in the hot Moroccan sun like fine gems. We walked past groups of nut-brown, black-eyed laughing children begging for dirhams. The guide said, 'Don't give. If you give to one you have to give to them all.' My husband pulled out all the change he had and we watched their smiles. We heard chanting from tall minarets and watched the faithful rush, a stream of humanity, in front of the Panorama Hotel. In the Jemaa el Fna square, our senses beat to the drums of the dancers. The snake charmers and medicine men topsy-turvied our reason.

The shadowy newsreel continues. Jewish men, dark-hatted, some with side locks and long black coats, tired women with bundles that are babies and tremulous children, stumble painfully through icy wastes to woods outside Riga. There they are forced to strip naked in the chill, still whiteness of Bikernieker Forest. My grandfather was the Chief Rabbi of Germany at the time of Hitler. He was told to flee, but he felt his place was with his congregants. He rode the cattle trains giving succour to those who knew their fate, or suspected that they would be murdered.

I have heard the words. Know the truth – been told the story as a growing-up child hears the legends, about her grandpa and her grandma, her aunties and uncles, cousins she has never seen, except as set photos of smiling people in sepia lives. It is my childhood, my adolescence. I have heard that this place Bikernieker forest outside Riga is where my grandfather was murdered, along with four hundred Jews.

The newsreel runs on. I sit in a hotel in Marrakech and I feel their fear, their humiliation. One is too slow. He is pushed with the butt of a bayonet. There are guns to their heads. The men are made to dig the icy earth and form their own graves. Polished jackboots kick.

The newsreel finishes. One of those men was my grandfather. He lay in the cold and the ice with no one to hold him or love him, or kiss his frost-bitten fingers, or wrap his chill, exposed, private person.

My written world has goose-stepped into my lived existence. The waxing veneer of time and 'then', had kept me unscathed. But today, my comfort blanket of 'now' has been dragged from my hands, from the suck of my mouth. In my mind I have nowhere to go. Seconds more and I would have seen my grandfather murdered with his fellow martyrs. The newsreel stopped. And yet it runs on in my mind, on and on – the video rewind of those ghostly moments, mine to keep, to rerun, no protection, no relief.

My husband wakes. 'You OK, love? You look ...?'

'Yes. Yes. I'm fine,' I say.

'I could do with a drink. Wonderful sleep. You sleep so relaxed here. Don't you? An hour outside? Take your writing?'

Back in the darkened garden in Marrakech, the fountains clink magenta diamonds of light and sound. Clouds of green and gold finches that flew in to roost in the oasis of rich purple bougainvilleas, date palms and bugles of red hibiscus, twitter contentment. In the background we hear faint strains of oriental music. The air is scented with evening jasmine, roses and orange blossom. We sit together. He orders French coffee. He admires the vivid blue-violet of the Jacaranda tree.

'I'd like to buy one of those,' he says. 'I wonder if it would grow at home.'

BIOGRAPHY

Ruth Joseph dreamt of writing fiction when she worked as a freelance journalist for IPC magazines. She has always been passionate in her crusade against cruelty and holds the belief that the essential qualities for the survival of the human race are love and tolerance. Her childhood and teenage years were spent as a carer for her Jewish anorexic mother and as a result, her life rotated around feasting and starving.

Her prize-winning stories reflect her philosophy and have been published in numerous anthologies, including Parthian, Honno, Loki, and Cambrensis. New Welsh Review and The Western Mail Magazine have also published her work.

She also had a cookery book published before obtaining a Master of Philosophy degree in Writing from Glamorgan University.

She lives in Cardiff with her husband Mervyn, daughter Sarah, son Jolyon, son-in-law Darren, granddaughters Jasmine and Phoebe, and rescued labrador Bobbi. She enjoys classical music, painting and flea-market trips as well as walking in her local park.

Other Titles
From Accent Press Ltd

The 'Shorts' range of charity books.

Accent Press Ltd produces two 'Shorts' charity books each year. Each book contains shorts stories that are donated by writers, including many 'big names', and raises £1 per copy sold for charity. The stories are 'naughty but nice' and fit perfectly into the lives of today's busy reader.

Sexy Shorts for Christmas   ISBN 0954489918
In support of Breast Cancer Campaign Reg. charity # 299758

Sexy Shorts for Summer   ISBN 0954489934
In support of Cancer Research UK Reg. charity # 1089464

Scary Shorts for Halloween   ISBN 0954489942
In support of Breast Cancer Campaign Reg. charity # 299758

…and coming soon

Sexy Shorts for Lovers   January 2005
In support of British Heart Foundation Reg. charity # 225971

Sexy Shorts for Students   October 2005
Charity to be confirmed

More Titles
From Accent Press Ltd

Why Do You Overeat?   ISBN 0954489993
When All You Want Is To Be Slim   £9.99
Author Zoë Harcombe has spent twenty years researching
the causes of over-eating. The result is this book, which
explains the three reasons why people struggle to lose
weight. Finally a diet book which works – long-term.

Notso Fatso   ISBN 0954489969
Walter Whichelow   £6.99
A tongue-in-cheek, ruthless and very funny take on the
world of dieting. Walter takes no prisoners as he explains
why there's only one way to lose weight – his way!

How to Draw Cartoons   ISBN 0954709209
Brian Platt   £7.99
Fun, simple and entertaining – this book will help even the
complete novice turn out professional cartoons in minutes.
Suitable for all ages.

Triplet Tales   ISBN 0954709217
Hazel Cushion & Brian Platt   £4.99
The first in a delightful series following triplets through
their early years. Beautifully written in rhyming couplets
with full colour illustrations by internationally published
cartoonist, Brian Platt. This book is sure to be a children's
favourite. (AVAILABLE NOV 2004)

Titles Available By Post

To order titles from Accent Press Ltd by post, simply tick the titles you wish to purchase, complete the form below and return to the address below, enclosing a cheque or postal order for the full amount plus £1 p&p per book.

	TITLE	AUTHOR	
☐	Sexy Shorts for Christmas	Various	£6.99
☐	Sexy Shorts for Summer	Various	£6.99
☐	Scary Shorts for Halloween	Various	£6.99
☐	Why Do You Overeat? When All You Want Is To Be Slim	Zoë Harcombe	£9.99
☐	How to Draw Cartoons	Brian Platt	£7.99
☐	Notso Fatso	Walter Whichelow	£6.99
☐	Triplet Tales (Nov 2004)	Hazel Cushion	£4.99

All prices correct at time of going to press. However the publisher reserves the right to change prices without prior notice.

Accent Press Ltd, PO Box 50, Pembroke Dock
Pembrokeshire, UK. SA72 6WY
Email: info@accentpress.co.uk Tel: + 44 (0) 1646 691389

Payments can be made by cheque or postal order made payable to Accent Press Ltd. Do not send cash or currency. Credit/ debit cards are not accepted.

NAME

ADDRESS

POSTCODE